Year of the Bear

For Cass; you are the best thing that's ever been mine.

Jay Chesters

First published in Australia 2022 by YndFwd (Slf Pty Ltd)

Cataloguing-in-Publication entry is available from the National Library of Australia http://catalogue.nla.gov.au

First Published in Great Britain 2022 by YndFwd Limited

A CIP catalouge record for this book
is available from the British Library

www.yndfwd.com/Publishing

Contents

March of the Bears

It was the year of the bear. After the bushfires came back-to-back once-in-a-thousand-year storms and floods, then the global pandemic, and then sometimes all of it at once.

Then, after the pandemic, the bears.

They numbered in their thousands, maybe hundreds of thousands. There seemed to be more every time you looked.

Impossible to distinguish one from another, the bears pressed together and moved with a single purpose and a single mind.

They clogged the roads and the streets. Nobody had ever seen so many bears. Nobody had guessed that so many bears even still survived in the country. Yet they were undeniable; a growing, teaming mass of bear—black bears, grizzly bears, brown bears, and everything in between—all lumbering along, oblivious to everything else.

Occasionally a fight would break out, and two enormous beasts would rise up on their back legs with a deafening roar. Even people who had begun to creep outside their homes to watch would take a step back, afraid that some spell would be broken and the bears would notice them, turn on them. But they never did. And the fights rarely came to any actual violence; there might be a swipe of a giant paw, or an enormous set of teeth would graze an opponent, but it would be forgotten almost as soon as it began.

We couldn't tell if they were running from something or towards it. The truth is, the bears didn't seem to be in any great hurry to be anywhere, but their numbers grew every day, with every town they passed through, always more bears.

It was almost an unspoken agreement that we wouldn't touch them, interfere with them, hurt them. We didn't know when it started, but it showed no signs of stopping.

The Ring Bearer

I sat in my underwear, watching the wedding as it played on my laptop in real-time. Yesterday's beer bottles stood guard on the coffee table.

Camera off, Zoom window pinned in the corner of the screen, I was distractedly switching tabs, scouring Pinterest for web design inspiration. Maybe I could design something featuring bears? Bears were in this season.

Bears had started appearing outside car dealership sale events or with a TV weather forecaster under hot studio lights.

While I searched for sourdough advice and foraging deals on pre-worn iconic Levi jeans, the wedding continued in its corner. The celebrant was more a droning burr than anything else but doing an excellent job of moving things along. He probably had several other events to do that day.

There was strange normalcy to virtual ceremonies. It had become usual for weekends to have a Zoom wedding, a child's baptism on Microsoft Teams, a funeral broadcast live on IGTV. Virtual events meant avoiding crowds, almost limitless guests, and no catering costs.

The groom was wearing flannel and had trimmed their iso-beard for the occasion. Was the wedding's theme 'ironic hillbilly' or 'retro lumberjack'? I couldn't tell from the guests, so I minimised Pinterest's inspirational mood boards to better concentrate on the fuzzy event video.

I wouldn't miss something only to be asked about it in the reception's YouTube channel. Making quiet and occasional chuffs, shifting his feet slightly, or giving a flick of an ear at a passing insect, the ring bearing bear was bearing up surprisingly well.

A member of the wedding party started reading a poem. She was sitting at home at her kitchen table in a Rockabilly bridesmaid's dress, her earnest words slightly muffled by the buzz of her fridge.

I stopped daydreaming and started paying attention to the wedding, however virtual.

The couple's vows were taking on new significance, *in sickness and in health* and *'till death do us part* now felt conspicuous under an ongoing global pandemic's cloud.

Then came exchanging rings. The ring bearer, whose luscious coat had been so lovingly brushed for the occasion, stepped forward on cue.

What came next will be analysed for decades. Some say there was a bee in the bride's bouquet, others insist the bear panicked when the celebrant cut the ribbon holding the couple's rings.

The celebrant was unceremoniously torn asunder, and the fleeing social media savant and their oversized laptop were no match for a grisly 200-kilo predator.

Eley's Revolver

Eley isn't moving.

But there isn't much of him left to move.

My ears are ringing, a juvenile bear lies bleeding on the carpet, and I'm not about to hang around for some interfering cops to show up.

It all went down something like this: For weeks, Eley had been promising me he had the goods, promising me he had a fortune in blood diamonds. Promising until he was blood red in the face.

The deal was supposed to be bloodless. From my side, anyway. A fortune in cash for a fortune in diamonds I could easily clean. I've earned a reputation that means people don't tend to mess around, and I don't usually waste my time with people like Eley.

Now Eley is dead, a bear is bleeding all over the place, and here I am with a loaded gun and a stolen car.

But I'm getting ahead of myself.

***

He was petulant like a teenager. Any time Eley thought someone else had things better than he did, you'd see a particular expression, hard and cruel, fall over his face like a shroud.

He'd always had an attitude like a spoilt child. Eley didn't just want to eat his cake and have it; he wanted to eat his cake, have his cake, and have your cake, too, in case your cake was better.

Once, Eley heard a rumour about how a rival kept a live tiger in a cage at their house. Eley was furious because he'd only ever kept dangerous dogs, although trained specifically for cruelty.

Eley wanted a wild animal, too, and before you knew it, he had a juvenile brown bear living in his house, occasionally attacking people.

***

Eley had that same black look on his face as he pointed the gun at me, impatiently chewing his gum.

He wanted me to drink the whiskey, which he'd clearly spiked or poisoned.

Of course, Eley was double-crossing me; he probably presumed I'd change my mind or I'd double-cross him, too.

Someone as disloyal as Eley always presumes everyone else is as much of a coward as they are. That's why he thought a life of crime was a get-rich-quick scheme and why he was every bit of an abject failure at being a career criminal.

That's not to say I expected his double cross precisely like this, but I was unsurprised. And I was prepared.

I should have been scared, but that's my secret.

***

They say that dogs can smell fear. It's not so much the emotion they smell as it is a specific hormone in your sweat.

The thing people don't often mention is that bears can smell it, too. The only real difference between the animals is that you don't want to be close enough to a bear to realise it smells your fear. If you are, it's too late to do anything other than be afraid.

I was unafraid, even with Eley childishly pointing his gun at me. I could tell he was scared and irrational enough to use the thing. I expect he probably knew how to use it—but he was always the kind of person that talks too much when they're nervous. His hands were shaking; he'd probably never fired the revolver at anything more dangerous than a rabbit caught in a fence.

What difference it made if I drank his spiked whiskey, I'm willing to bet, was that Eley hoped to not have to shoot me when I was still conscious. He couldn't guarantee he'd kill me if he did—I don't think his aim was good enough—and if Eley didn't kill me, then he knew my reputation. He knew what I could do.

As Eley tightly gripped his gun, I couldn't help but giggle. This felt ridiculous. He thought being a crime boss was all about double-crossing the other guy, whiskey bottles and magnum .45s. He probably tried wearing a fedora hat at some point too.

Eley didn't get that most of the time the game is all tiny things that hardly anyone notices. A slight influence here. An insider there. A tip-off about some diamonds that happen to get redirected without anyone getting hurt. No real people, at least.

'What's so funny?' Eley asked.

But the bear could smell the fear on him and knew something was going down. Before I could reply, it attacked, Eley's gun went off, and, at that moment, the cramped, messy study felt like a giant had picked up the house and was shaking it to watch the snow fall inside.

***

If he hadn't accidentally shot the bear, I doubt any of us would be here to tell the tale.

There was a moment when I walked in and first saw the bear. I was surprised but oddly unafraid. I knew the stories but was still surprised there really was a bear. Our eyes met, the bear and me.

I'm not saying we had an understanding, but I saw something expressed in the bear I thought I knew. I've always liked bears; something about them reminds me of my old man. It might be the contrast between their sad old eyes and how they can tear a man apart in seconds.

Perhaps that was why I left Eley on the carpet; I half dragged the unconscious bear out to Eley's car, heaved it into the passenger seat, started the engine, and turned up the radio.

I think this gets us up to date. Eley is dead, his bear is bleeding all over the place, I'm here with a loaded gun, speeding in a stolen car to the hospital. I have to get the bear help, and Eley's revolver will ensure they help me.

***

I practically abandon the car at the hospital. It's not exactly in front of the doors—I wouldn't want to block ambulance access, I'm not a monster—but I'm not about to find a suitable bay half a kilometre away and pay for parking.

I drag the bear indoors—while not fully grown, it's still heavier than most men, and I struggle, despite the adrenaline coursing through me. The patients and visitors react with a mix of horror and shock and fear and almost amusement. It's as if they're looking for a hidden camera like they're extras in some YouTube-Netflix collaboration, and they're ready to sign the release form and tell their friends.

The hospital staff are slightly less calm. Security is unamused but also clearly haven't trained for this. The orderlies don't get paid enough for dealing with people dragging bleeding, unconscious bears into their hospital.

From the receptionist's blood-drained face, it looks like he'd prefer to pretend this isn't happening, and he's busy pretending his style magazine is essential business.

'My friend here needs help urgently', I say.

'Your ... your friend?' the receptionist sputters.

'Yes. My friend has got a bullet in him, and if he doesn't get help, he's going to die right here while these people with their bloody noses and their sprained ankles watch.'

'But ... your friend ... is a bear. We're not a veterinary hospital.'

In that moment, I'm tempted to reply with something sarcastic. However, the receptionist is beyond subtlety, and the delay isn't helping anyone.

Instead, I point Eley's revolver at him. My hands don't shake, and I'm not afraid to use a gun to get what I need.

The security guards get busy calling in the threat. Since they don't come armed, they're just going to do whatever it takes not to startle me into shooting other patients.

'I don't have time to mess around, and I don't have time to find an exotic pet vet that deals with ursine gunshot wounds. Either you help my friend, or your doctors are going to become the west coast's specialists in bullet extractions.'

This seems to do the trick. Before I know it, three burly orderlies are lifting the bear onto a trolley, and I follow them, despite various protests.

This isn't over.

And sure, I wanted to get away from Eley's before the cops showed up; what do I think will happen now?

Maybe it's not always about the small things after all. But between the bear, me, the diamonds, the cash, and Eley's revolver, I've got a feeling we're all going to be okay.

So long as the bear lives.

The Moon Bear

Sam awoke with a headache like a mythical curse. Fittingly, he'd also transformed into a grizzly bear.

This wasn't unusual; Sam changed every quarter on the full moon closest to the equinox. This made it difficult to predict them precisely without a calendar, making it difficult for him to practise as a personal injury lawyer.

Some clients were startled by a bear in their meetings, even when he'd vainly tried wearing a tie. Not everyone was happy with him managing their case; people sometimes acted like they couldn't understand his gruff voice. Others just rudely demanded someone else.

Sam's bosses didn't mind—his transformations only lasted a day or two and had their advantages: although during that time, completing paperwork was a struggle, at trial, his presence could be a bonus.

Sam was a very gentle soul and would never hurt anyone. Even in human form, he'd prefer to usher a fly out the door than swat one.

***

Sam was grateful that the Bear Moon fell on Easter weekend this quarter, giving him four days away from the office. Having worked late all week, he'd gone for Friday drinks with his colleagues to celebrate their wins, then headed home. Home to reheated Korean chicken takeaway and bingeing Netflix episodes of *Brave the Wild*.

Early Saturday morning, Sam tried wiping the sleep from his eyes before realising his paws were too big for such a delicate, human movement. With a pitiful growl, he climbed from the couch where he'd fallen asleep the night before as a human.

Sam now stood over 2 metres tall, and as he scratched his back against the door frame, he remembered something important: he had a date to keep.

He'd chatted all week to the alluring Alex on Tinder. Sam liked that she was fun and intelligent, and he was particularly taken by the freckles in her hazel eyes.

They'd arranged to meet at his favourite bar/café, but seeing himself in his full-length mirror, Sam had a problem. He'd been so busy with work he'd forgotten to look at a calendar when arranging the date and couldn't very well show up looking like he did now. He hadn't mentioned to Alex his metamorphosis, a minor lapse in judgement he was regretting now.

Being a large grizzly bear meant Sam's designer distressed jeans and band T-shirt wouldn't fit. He'd also realised early on in his professional life that bears wearing clothes look ridiculous; people made jokes about the circus and Sam's temper was short in his fine ursine form.

Sam didn't want to cancel; he was looking forward to meeting Alex. Besides, the Sorry, turned into a bear excuse was lame; she probably heard it all the time.

But, he wasn't going to turn up with knotted fur. He had a better idea: Sam was friends with the owner of the local dog wash. A couple of years ago, he'd represented her when she'd been injured at work—her resulting compensation had helped her open her business.

***

An hour later, after an affectionate wash and brushing and scaring an elderly Italian couple's French poodle, Sam was ready for his date.

There weren't many places bear-Sam could go, and the irony wasn't lost on him that his preferred bar was called The Moon, but he could smell the host's discomfort when he arrived.

'I have a booking for 5 pm?' Sam's question was unclear, sounding like growling to the annoyed host's impatient ears.

'Shoo! Leave our bins alone!' they snapped back.

When people deliberately didn't understand him, Sam would stand on his hind legs and yawn rather than perform an elaborate pantomime. So that's what he did.

Faced with jaws almost as wide as his head, the host nearly fainted. Being a bear had advantages. Sam wandered in and climbed into a booth near the back.

***

Sam told Alex in advance how his favourite spot was at the back and to expect a surprise. When she arrived, Sam caught the spike in pheromones as their eyes met and he had a good feeling. Sometimes, his dates weren't pleased to encounter bears, but Alex almost smouldered.

Sharing their fries and swapping stories, their conversation sparkled like salmon in a stream. Alex didn't always understand Sam right away, but she'd spent a summer with bears in Alaska's Katmai National Park and quickly picked up the subtleties when he was talking.

Alex was smart and funny, and the date felt effortless. Sam was wound around Alex's little finger, and he could tell she liked him too. It was going all a little too well, and that made Sam uneasy. He needed to be honest.

'I want to say something', Sam started.

'If it's that you turn into a bear, I think I guessed that. But maybe mention it in your Tinder bio?' Alex pointed at Sam with her slice of pizza almost accusingly, but she was smiling.

While sometimes Sam felt braver as a bear, sometimes he felt like he had more to hurt. Hurt feelings weren't something allowed in his line of work.

'It's OK,' Alex reassured him, 'I'm not mad. Bears are better than some people.' Sam's ears perked up, and his fur seemed to glisten.

'What did you want to tell me?' Alex asked.

'My work ... can be a dealbreaker', Sam started, cautiously.

'Bears have jobs?' Alex teased.

'Don't say the circus!' Sam shot back, jostling his pint, spilling some on his fur. 'You know I'm not a bear all the time; it's only a few times a year', Sam shot back, good-naturedly. 'Those are my real photos! I visited Machu Picchu in 2019, and I go rock climbing every week.'

Alex was curious; she hadn't thought about how Sam's bear-form affected his hobbies. 'Does being a bear help?'

'Not indoors, at a gym. Some places don't like me coming in, and those artificial walls aren't designed for bears. I prefer a weekend in the karri forests near Pemberton.'

'You must scare the tourists.'

'I go in winter and keep to myself', Sam reassured her. 'As a bear, I can hear and smell people a long way away, so it's easy.'

'Can you smell me?' Alex asked, unsure.

'In the city, and a place like this, the world is an olfactory orchestra. An orchestra with every instrument playing at once.'

'That wasn't no', Alex laughed.

Sam enjoyed her humour; she had a cheeky streak as broad as the purple-red lines in her scruffy blonde hair. 'Can we get back on topic?' he asked carefully.

Alex sat up straight. 'Right, of course, Mr Sam. Please tell me about this Important Business that's much more important than another drink.'

'My business card says personal injury lawyer.'

The playful light went from Alex's eyes. 'An ambulance chaser', she said flatly. It wasn't a question.

'That's offensive', Sam almost growled.

'And I am leaving', Alex replied, standing up and grabbing her jacket. 'See you around.'

'I hold people accountable for their actions', Sam almost whispered. He didn't often defend his work: if people didn't like it, they didn't have to. But he liked Alex.

'I've seen the ads on TV: *no win, no fee*', Alex said. She had put her jacket on but hadn't attempted to leave yet. 'I get lawyers circling the café at the hospital like sharks, convincing people to make claims.'

'Some people have a lawyer they know they can call on, a friend or a family member. But I work with people new to the country, often less well-off people who don't know any lawyers. I pride myself on being caring and honest; I want to help.'

Sam heaved a big bear sigh, and Alex seemed to visibly soften. She reached out and stroked his fur.

'I see where you're coming from.'

Walking her outside, Sam waited with Alex for her ride home, ignoring the looks of passers-by. When her ride finally arrived she hugged him goodbye, gave him an unexpectedly big kiss between the eyes, and with an 'I'll text you!' she was away.

***

Running home, Sam loved being a bear tonight, with the breeze in his fur and the air smelling of citrus.

Once home, he stretched out on the living room floor, exhausted. Before he could fall asleep, his mobile beeped with a message.

'Hi, Sam, safely home', it read.

Sam had a feeling he might know why Alex was warming to him.

'You do know nothing can happen between us when I'm like this?' Sam asked, gesturing to himself with his enormous bear paws, even though he was alone.

What followed surprised him more.

'I like you,' Alex explained, 'but I'm not into bears like *that*. I mean, I'm not going to lie and say it doesn't help because you can only date so many guys in band T-shirts before they're all the same. But, we wouldn't have matched on Tinder at all if I didn't like you as a person. Can I see you again, Friday?'

You Awake to Find Yourself in a Dark Room

In the dark, something starts moving.

The offer: $50,000 to escape the room. Easy money, so I thought.

What's made me a winner, over and over and over again, is breaking things down. One expectation. One misconception. It's all one more problem to solve.

There could be a thousand things before my door opens, but I don't need to solve thousands: only one. One problem, one thousand times over.

The door isn't a problem right now. Number one: find the light switch.

This place is darker than a crypt at midnight. I can't see anything, but my other senses are tools I do have.

Start with touch. It's bloody cold in here, I don't even need to touch anything to know that. I need to keep moving.

The walls are my first surprise. I expect smooth plaster, as blank and featureless as my conscience. Instead, they're rough, jagged like rock. Damp to the touch. Kneeling, the floor is slightly wet, too.

'This is a twist', I mutter. 'They've gone big with this budget.'

Or else I wasn't far off when I mentioned a crypt.

A secret: what makes me the worldwide number one escapee is not relying on any single piece of info. It's listing what I know. And what do I know so far? There's nothing to see, and this room isn't a room.

What else? It smells damp, like brackish water. I can hear it trickling down the walls. And something else, too. It smells like everything else but stronger—like something in here smells *more* than the damp.

Nothing is an accident in these places. That doesn't mean everything is significant— sometimes they're red herrings, but they aren't accidental. What can I do with this olfactory information?

Any smells won't help me find a light, but then again, maybe there isn't a light? I wouldn't put it past them to keep me in the dark.

I can see something. Now my eyes have adjusted, I can see my breath, like the wisp of a ghost. This tells me my body is warmer than the air, and if I don't find a way out, I'll be in trouble.

Trouble isn't new, inside a room or outside. I don't need to look for trouble; it's waiting for me every day when I open my eyes.

The walls feel slightly mossy in places. This tells me something else useful: this room hasn't been constructed for my escape, it's pre-existing.

I can probably assume the room won't fill with water because the water is a natural feature. Together, the water and the moss tell me this place is old.

They add peril to these escapes for the big prizes. Because it's a peril room the time limit is how long it takes me to die from the cold. Combined with the dark, this kind of stacking of perils isn't cheating, only frowned upon.

What else would I expect for $50,000, though? A couple of number puzzles and an anagram? This isn't a crossword competition.

I can't see anything else, and I don't plan to taste anything, so that leaves me with what I can hear. I hold my breath and stop moving, list the things I can hear: A faint trickle of water on the walls. Infrequent drips.

Sometimes what you can't hear tells you more. There's no ticking clock— that's added to increase pressure, to get in your head. What does that tell me? They don't need to get in my head. *Fuck.*

That does what it's intended: they aren't trying to increase the pressure because they're confident, and that does get to me. There's no simple ploy to mess with me, so this will be difficult. Maybe it's the cold and the dark already getting to me.

This unusual choice of room has got me on edge, too. There's no hum of electricity or a generator of any kind. I can stop looking for a light switch— there isn't an electric light.

With no artificial time limit I should explore my confines. I don't know how big the room is, so I'll follow the wall around.

I need a marker that will tell me when I'm back at the start, help me find my way. Ariadne hasn't given me a ball of thread for this labyrinth, so I improvise. I take off my T-shirt and tear a strip from it.

Around head height there's enough of a notch to tie the fabric to; that will do. It's important to have something like this. Outsmart them.

Creeping along the wall, I stumble once or twice; the floor is as rough and uneven as the walls. I was wrong before. This isn't a crypt, or something made of blocks of stone. It would be obvious, feeling the walls. No. This is a cave.

It's clever, but it could be their undoing—there are multiple ways out of a cave. They shook me, but this restores my confidence. This is why I'm the champ.

The wall is too slippery to climb in the dark, and the occasional cracks and crevices reveal nothing. No torches. No gas lamps. No doorways. My hands are numb. I must have been walking for almost 30 minutes, though in surroundings like this it's impossible to know how far I've gone.

The cold is soaking into my bones. It feels like—*wait*. I hear something. I thought it was my imagination, the sound of my breathing. But there it is again. I've been so preoccupied with trying to see, despite myself, that I wasn't paying attention.

Something is breathing. Something with large lungs and a guttural rattle. It's breathing deeply, easily. Peacefully.

Nobody mentioned I'd have company. It's more unnerving than a ticking death row clock.

Whatever they are, I don't think they know I'm here. I need to get out before they do.

As soon as I think I need to be careful, I trip and fall onto a large bulky body.

***

'Contestant 1334, our undefeated challenger, fails to escape Bear Room.'

Bear room? The sudden announcement, booming from hidden speakers, startles and almost deafens me. The bear is undoubtedly awake now.

The announcement continues: 'The title is still up for grabs for anyone who wants to earn their freedom and $50,000.'

Love Listens with its Eyes

This Wednesday was cold for July, and the gallery's midday tour was quieter than usual. Jorge wondered how many of the other guests had only wandered into the Tate only to warm up and visit the gift shop.

Jorge visited the converted power station on the south bank of the muddy river Thames on days he felt like he didn't belong at art school. Once there, he'd join one of Tate Modern's free daily guided tours instead of going to his lectures.

He didn't mind what displays the tours visited; he just loved hearing what different tour guides liked so much, and it reminded him of why he was studying fine art.

One surprisingly elderly lady named Margot talked passionately on tours about how the artist Stezaker used collage to significant effect. She said she thought it was 'quite wonderful' how he combined found objects and everyday materials.

Another guide, whom he thought of as 'the brigadier' for his military-like bearing and fearsome moustache, favoured Stephen Shore's 'genuinely groundbreaking' work in his *American Surfaces* series.

Among the five other visitors on his *Making Sense of Modern Art* tour, Jorge recognised one particular guest and noticed how she occasionally pulled a notebook out of her dusty canvas messenger bag to make notes from the artwork labels. She looked familiar, and Jorge was intrigued by how her cropped red hair covered her ears, but he knew they'd not spoken before.

The tour finished, and as the other visitors drifted away to buy their postcards and coasters, Jorge was left with the familiar red-haired notetaker. Together they were admiring the same expressionist painting of a woman sitting side by side on a bed with what looked like a grizzly bear.

The picture's subject looked off to one side, and the bear rested one enormous paw on her shoulder. Jorge could almost feel a gulf of silence between the two figures. Or perhaps the bear was comforting the woman?

Their perceived silence felt as imposing and out of place as the painting's bear.

'Do those guides really know what they're talking about?' Jorge offered, without turning from the painting.

He was half-serious but smiling, and a pang of panic began growing when his companion didn't answer. Maybe she was a tour guide, and he'd offended her? Or perhaps she found it best to ignore odd and accented strangers.

If he could help it, Jorge rarely asked questions on tours or even in lectures. English wasn't his first language.

Jorge had gone to schools in several countries. He was confident writing essays on dozens of subjects but still self-conscious talking. His accent echoed mockingly in his ears, and he often worried he'd say something wrong—like mispronouncing *Worcestershire*, or 'my hovercraft is full of eels.'

Not knowing what else to do, Jorge continued talking; 'I mean, of course, they know what they're talking about. But art is so subjective … don't you think?'

Turning to Jorge with a small sigh and without speaking, the young woman by his side reached into her messenger bag and pulled out a battered notepad and pen. Jorge was briefly confused.

On the pad was a single line she'd written: *Hi, my name is Clare, and I'm deaf—if you'd like to chat, we can use my notepad.*

It was the most beautiful thing Jorge had ever seen, and it was Clare's handwriting he first loved.

Clare offered Jorge her pad and pen with a polite smile. He readily accepted before realising how idiotic he'd sound writing down his inane thoughts. Instead, he introduced himself and offered to leave her in peace.

I don't mind company, Claire wrote back. *If you don't mind written conversations?*

They spent the next few hours together, wandering the other galleries, content sharing silence, with Clare occasionally writing comments to Jorge. *Not sure about this one*, she'd offer, or a simple observation like *This makes me feel sad.*

Eventually, Clare complained to Jorge that her feet were sore, and she was going for a coffee. She invited Jorge to join her, and he enthusiastically accepted. Jorge then immediately worried his enthusiasm made his handwriting untidy.

Next to Clare's, Jorge thought his handwriting looked like a drunken spider had been dipped into ink and allowed to wander happily across a page. Clare didn't seem to notice, or maybe she didn't mind.

Over their coffees, Clare and Jorge learnt they were in some of the same classes at University of the Arts London, and then as if they'd already known each other for years, they were friends. For what felt like a very long time, Jorge didn't think of Clare as anything else.

Clare and Jorge continued meeting on days they shared the same classes and spent most evenings together watching old films. One of the first times they'd met for coffee together, Clare had told Jorge that she could lip-read but often found it frustrating and exhausting. She lamented that people would talk to her without looking at her—Jorge quietly blushed, and Clare pretended not to notice—or they didn't enunciate properly.

Once, she'd spent several frustrating hours sitting around uncomfortably in Accident & Emergency. She'd later learned the doctor had been calling her name with his back turned to her.

What about sign language? Jorge had asked her, and Clare smiled kindly. 'Do you speak BSL?' she signed for him, slowly. Embarrassed, Jorge admitted he had no idea what she was saying.

Didn't think so, Clare wrote. Many people don't. I don't blame you, you weren't born here and learning English must be hard. And so, it was agreed, Clare would help Jorge learn sign language.

Jorge asked once if Clare minded that more people didn't learn BSL. She'd shrugged as if to say, 'yeah, but what can you do?' though she reassured Jorge that how you communicate was less important than trying.

Many people avoid or ignore deaf people because they're afraid to try, she said.

The classic films and cheesy rom-coms they watched together always had subtitles, and Jorge soon found that he appreciated English-language films more if he could read as well as watch them.

Sometimes, Clare would mercilessly tease him about the various boys he was dating or bringing home. When Jorge tried to argue, she'd hold the notepad behind her back so he couldn't reply.

***

Jorge and Clare were friends for more than a year before Jorge learnt why she always wore her hair covering her ears, and in that moment, Jorge thought his heart would break.

One night on Claire's three-seater couch, they shared a bottle of wine and chatted, just the two of them. It was tradition, what they always did when Jorge was fresh out of a relationship and feeling sorry for himself.

Having sworn this latest one was the one, Jorge was in a funk. Browsing the internet on his laptop without really looking, he claimed he was hunting for inspiration. Inspiration for what, he didn't say. Clare's use of the 'face with raised eyebrow' emoji in their Messenger conversation gently suggested that while she wasn't calling him a liar, she also didn't believe him.

Clare was engrossed reading a tattered pulp paperback Western when Jorge gently tapped her on the knee, interrupting her gunslingers. Wordlessly, he was saying he wanted to show her something. Passing Clare his laptop, she read the heartwarming story of a dad who got tattoos of cochlear implants so his deaf five-year-old son could feel normal.

Jorge wondered why Clare didn't pass the laptop back almost right away; there wasn't that much of the story to read. He'd been careful to close his open tabs first, and he didn't think Clare would start reading other articles. Jorge was sitting patiently at first, but then his mind began suggesting things she might find in his emails or his browsing history, and he started to fidget. Jorge was about to make an excuse and ask for it back when Clare began typing.

Jorge looked at Clare quizzically, his head to one side

'What's wrong?' he signed, clumsily.

Nobody would ever tell him, but people often thought Jorge looked like a disgruntled Labrador when he did this. Perhaps it was his brown eyes, but he looked like a chubby yellow lab, upset about not getting food.

Clare had clearly seen Jorge looking at her but carried on typing regardless—before stopping abruptly and passing over the laptop without looking his way. Jorge knew she was upset, and for a moment worried he'd made her mad.

There was a sudden knot in his stomach, though he had no idea why he felt like the room was growing stiflingly hot. Then he read what Clare wrote.

She described how she'd had a cochlear implant many years ago and thought it would change her life. *Not that simple*, she'd written. *It's not magic. If you're born deaf, your brain needs to be trained *how* to hear. If learning BSL is hard, try learning how to *hear*.*

I cried in secret every night for weeks, I thought I was broken and didn't want anyone to know. Before the operation, I was so hopeful that I'd miraculously be able to hear. Instead, all I got was an excruciating buzzing.

The doctors tried telling me it wasn't uncommon. 'Some bodies reject implants', they said. I felt like it was my fault for not trying hard enough. It was as if my implant had rejected me as a person because I was unworthy.

As Jorge read Clare's hurt and disappointment, he didn't immediately notice how she now held her hair back for him to see her scars.

At that moment, as he looked up, he understood—and understood he had been hopelessly and unhesitatingly in love with Clare for months.

***

It was a grey and drizzly Sunday morning. They'd been doing charcoal sketches of photos from a glossy coffee table book of wildlife photography. He'd sketched a tiny fox, dwarfed by the snowy landscape around it, and Jorge remembered feeling ambivalent about his shading.

Clare's sketch of a grizzly bear was stunning, with fur that seemed almost like you could touch it and a sense of sadness in its eyes.

Jorge remembered how they'd both been looking at the same painting of the woman and bear after the gallery tour on the day they met. Something unnameable had changed in his feelings for Clare.

***

By their final year, they'd kissed briefly—once—while uncharacteristically drunk one evening. Jorge would never forget it; it felt funny kissing a face without stubble.

Clare later claimed she didn't remember that night, blaming the espresso martini cocktails. But to Jorge, the brush of her soft lips felt like the charcoal strokes of her sketch, and he was deeply besotted.

Some weeks later, on the night before their final exam, Jorge and Clare were in the studio late. They both turned to drawing when they felt stressed, and Clare likened it to pre-race training for a marathon. She said some runners would eat a large pasta meal the night before a race, so it was important to channel their own stress and anxiety into art.

Except Jorge couldn't concentrate on drawing. Some otherworldly force compelled him to tell Clare his feelings. Though he'd sworn never to tell her, he'd been turning it over in his mind recently, following a friend's car accident that had shaken up everyone.

As much as Jorge wanted to concentrate on his timber wolf, all he could think of were all the things he could say, stumbling over how to start. It wasn't like he could just give a cough and start talking.

'Clare, I need to speak to you' sounded too formal to him in BSL, like a command. Writing simply *Hey Clare, got a sec?* in her notebook sounded like he wanted her help moving furniture.

Clare stood up before Jorge could find the right words, signing to him that she was off to the pub.

'*Want to come?*' she asked.

As well as slightly clumsy BSL, the two of them had also developed a personal shorthand of actions over the years, a kind of sign language slang. Clare said she did the same with her family and that she had various actions specific to certain groups you wouldn't learn in any sign language classes.

With a dramatic swish of her coat, Clare was gone before Jorge could register what had happened.

He worked late into the night. Not on his pencil drawing of the enormous wolf—Jorge tried many times, without success, to capture the passion and life of Claire's wildlife sketches. Instead, he wrote her a love note in his neatest handwriting.

Jorge's 'note' was more like a letter, and though he kept it to one page, he rewrote it many times. Finally, it was close to midnight when he was done, and Jorge knew he had to get home and sleep. Instead of delivering the letter to Clare in person, he weighted it down with her charcoal set. The gesture seemed significant.

His letter was grand and romantic and would have put Gabriel García Márquez to shame. Had she ever received it, Clare would have loved it.

***

That night, a curious cleaner would move Clare's charcoal set so slightly her letter would fall onto the floor. This small action changed everything, and Jorge's letter ended up under a bookcase, unread, where it stayed for two years.

Over the following weeks, Jorge was disappointed when Clare didn't reply to or mention his letter, but they remained best friends for the rest of their lives.

Jorge never resented Clare's partners nor felt slighted; he enjoyed her friendship too much and loved her in his own way. He also might never have met his husband if Clare had acknowledged the letter and was often glad things worked out that way.

***

Jorge's letter resurfaced almost exactly 24 months later. Students moving furniture in the studio shifted a bookcase, and an aspiring artist named Claire found the uncovered letter the next day, mistakenly thinking it was for her.

Signed with only a J, Claire misinterpreted it as coming from her friend Julia and was quietly thrilled. She'd been grappling with her own fears and attractions for as long as she could remember.

To Claire, Julia seemed impossibly confident, and she'd endlessly debated with herself if she was in love with Julia or just wanted to be Julia. Julia, with her cuffed jeans and scuffed converse and her opinions and knowledge about everything and everyone in the art world.

But she hadn't ever considered doing anything about those feelings until now.

Clearly, she thought, Julia didn't want to risk confessing her feelings face to face. And so, Claire resolved to ask Julia on a date. It was terrifying, but one of them had to do it.

***

Years later, at a birthday party, Julia was briefly confused when Claire had mentioned a note. She meant to ask Claire about it, but with a whirlwind of well-wishers, it slipped her mind, and Claire didn't mention it again.

Under her bed, Claire kept a box of memories—mementos from the first times she met particular people in her life. There were flyers from gigs and tickets to gallery exhibition openings, bottle caps and beer mats, and one slightly scuffed letter.

The Right To Arm Bears

A brief guide to names in this story

In Russian, names consist of a first name, patronymic, and surname. The patronymic is formed from the name of the father. Male patronymics usually end with -ich, and female patronymics usually end with -vna. Your relationship to and with a person also affects the way you address them.

These are how the forms are used throughout this story, taking as an example these scenarios for the Soviet and Russian biologist Ilya Ivanovich Ivanov:

- *Ivanov Ilya Ivanovich: When visiting a polling station and there are hundreds of people with the last name Ivanov*

- *Ivanov: How a prison guard refers to inmate Ivanov. Or a strict school teacher teaching their student Ivanov discipline. Also used if you want to show utter contempt for Ivanov.*

- *Ilya Ivanovich: Addressing Ivanov in a respectful and formal manner; Ivanov may be your manager, or a colleague with whom you have a very formal relationship.*

- *Ilya: Addressing Ivanov in a friendly way because you're friends, or he's a colleague with whom you have a more relaxed working relationship. Also used in a more formal setting as a way of showing you're Ivanov's superior.*

- *Alyosha: Addressing Ivanov in a very familiar or affectionate way, either because you're a relative, a close friend, or you're a colleague using it in an almost cheeky way to get Ivanov to do something for you.*

Characters

Alexey Pavlovich Tolyubev: a Soviet geneticist studying *Drosophila* (fruit flies)

Anastasia Sergeevna Bratko: a Soviet biologist, and an expert in cross-species genetics

Brodyaga: a Soviet official

Saponya: a Soviet official and Brodyaga's superior

Serge Ivanovich Koshmak: a Soviet cosmonaut

Oleg Makarovich Tereshchenko: a house painter

Ilya Ivanovich Ivanov: the controversial Soviet biologist, notorious for his attempts to create a human-ape hybrid

Vladimir Petrovich Demikhov: the Soviet scientist and organ transplantation pioneer who performed the transplantation of a heart into an animal, also known for his dog head transplants

Tardigrades: also known as water bears or moss piglets, eight-legged segmented micro-animals

***

On April 11 2019, the Beresheet spacecraft catastrophically slammed into the Moon's surface, contaminating the pristine lunar surface with thousands of living creatures from Earth.

Tardigrades, also known as water bears, are found in every climate on Earth in the most inhospitable conditions. They figuratively shrug their microscopic shoulders at attempts to kill them. Surviving temperature extremes from absolute zero to more than 100°C, tardigrades can also withstand extreme pressures, along with oxygen deprivation and starvation. In 2007, tardigrades survived the vacuum of space and lethal levels of cosmic radiation. They can even survive for more than a century without water.

The lunar tardigrade survivors have been without oxygen, water or food for less than a decade. Most people reasonably assume this is the first time bears have existed on a world other than Earth.

These people are wrong.

An investigative journalist digging through declassified Cold War documents recently uncovered a series of memos and reports relating to *Project Oruzhiye Medvedi*. The name roughly translates to *weapon bears*.

What follows is an incomplete account.

***

Soviet Animal Operations - 1954, Moscow

Alexey Pavlovich Tolyubaev likes fruit flies.

It's not necessarily something he mentions on a date, but Thomas Hunt Morgan's work and the unassuming Drosophila aspires him to greatness like naked cherubs to a Renaissance painter. Though Alexey has little time for paintings.

In certain unremarkable corridors and rooms of official buildings, Alexey has achieved a professional reputation for his unassuming work, which remains ground breaking on his chosen subjects to this day.

Alexey recognises the possibility in the common insects, and with his fruit flies he can do so much.

Because nobody expects to crush their capitalist rival with weaponised fruit flies, they leave Alexey in peace. He doesn't expect medals or accolades for his work, and he likes it this way. Instead, he thinks of himself like a fruit fly: unassuming and overlooked, but capable of greatness.

The official's visit to his cluttered lab disturbs Alexey. The man's clothes are smart and clean, as if he enjoys a generous income a scientist can't aspire towards.

But the man is more like a bear than a fruit fly, Alexey thinks. He is hairy and burly like a bear. Yet, while he shows no kindness to him, Alexey sees there's a softness in the man's eyes, as if the two of them could be something like friends in a different time.

Walking around Alexey's messy lab, the official inspects various pieces of equipment, carelessly picking items up and turning them over in his enormous paws while speaking in short, staccato sentences. He is talking about the pioneering work of Vladimir Demikhov.

Everyone knows about Comrade Demikhov's experiments. Not everyone approves. Alexey, however, is a pragmatic man. While Demikhov's work is sometimes shocking, he diplomatically tells the official he understands the importance of the work—sacrifices are necessary for advancing science.

'It is not about advancing science', the official replies, startling Alexey with his intensity. 'We must win this war and crush our great rival.'

Alexey is unclear how Demikhov's transplant procedures will do this, but doesn't share his misgivings with the bear in the room. He breathes in heavily instead. The official has a musky smell like a wet dog, even though his clothes seem clean. For the briefest moment, Alexey wonders if Demikhov might have done something unspeakable: what if he transplanted a man's head onto a bear? He quickly corrects himself for the absurdity of the idea. While the official is a large man, he's only that: a large man, and not a bear in man's clothing.

But while the idea that this official might not be wholly human is absurd, Alexey begins wondering if this is what he means by Demikhov's work helping win the war. Not even Ivanov, in his distasteful experiments years ago, tried creating human-bear hybrids.

'You want me to work with Comrade Demikhov.' It's not a question. He's suddenly sure that's what this visit is about, that and officials not understanding how vast the field of biology is. One scientist working with animals would be much the same as the next in their minds, the same way all painters are alike.

'You're getting the idea', the official responds with a smile.

This isn't the same thing as saying yes. He is to report to an office the following day, where they'll continue their conversation.

***

In his small apartment on the outskirts of Moscow, Alexey lay awake, counting cracks in the ceiling. Sleep often comes easily to him, but tonight his mind is preoccupied with wondering what the idea is. There's no purpose for fruit flies in Demikhov's work.

***

Alexey wants to look presentable for his meeting. He combs his hair, shaves his face with cold water, and presses a clean shirt. When he doesn't know who he's meeting or what they want, he should assume the character of the model citizen.

Arriving early, he's unsurprised that the officials are running late, often the case with official meetings. More than once, he has speculated to himself if this is deliberate—like they want him to know how inferior he is. Except nobody needs to tell Alexey how inferior he is, he thinks. He knows he's barely more than a fly. But he's a useful fly today.

The official he met the day before is Comrade Brodyaga. His superior is Saponya. And they're talking about bears.

While they talk, Alexey's mind wanders. As a child, his grandmother often told him beautiful stories about bears—tales of clever bears, talking bears, and cunning bears. Alexey's favourite story was about a little girl named Masha, whom a talking bear forced to live in his house and work as his faithful servant. While in the story his grandmother told him, little Masha outwitted the bear, Alexey is sure he's heard a version where the child's fate is less happy.

The two officials are too impressed by their own cleverness and importance to notice when they ask him a question that their subject isn't paying attention. Alexey realises this puts him in a difficult position; he can't admit he doesn't know what they've been talking about.

The safest course of action is agreeing to whatever he's asked. Meetings of this kind are unlikely to be a suggestion or a request, so it matters little if he wants to go along with it.

'Very well', the official named Saponya announces. 'We will get you everything you need.'

'I will tell Comrade Bratko everything is in place. She will be pleased', Brodyaga adds; Saponya nods sternly. 'There is no time to waste; we will show you to your new laboratory and have it ready for you quickly.'

Alexey doesn't doubt agreeing is wise in these situations, but as he follows Brodyaga down the dimly lit corridor, he feels like he's a small goat being led away to market.

***

'I know who you are', the scientist named Anastasia Bratko tells Alexey when they're left alone after the boisterous introductions have been made.

Of course, Alexey knows who Anastasia is, too; everyone knows about her work on cross-species breeding. Alexey has seen pictures of Anastasia many times, but in person he's surprised how much gentler she seems. Her grey eyes are softer, she's a little shorter than he imagined, and he notices a small, dark red birthmark on her neck that he hasn't seen in any official photographs.

'I've also read your work', he admits, wisely keeping his other observations to himself. 'But I don't know what we're doing here, Anastasia Sergeevna. I work with fruit flies. And I don't do transplants.'

'Tolubaev, we are not here to do transplants. What do you think you're here for?'

'I told you already, I don't know. I agreed because there wasn't any other option.'

'Call me Anastasia', Alexey's now-partner replies. 'I'll explain everything.'

What follows seems more than outlandish to Alexey, and, if he didn't know better, he'd suspect Anastasia Bratko of making fun of him.

'They want us to breed an army?' he asks.

'Yes, it is to be an invading army of unstoppable proportions.'

'And it is an army … of intelligent bears?'

'Yes. They are large and fierce. The Americans will not expect to fight bears.' Anastasia seems almost delighted at the idea.

'I know nothing about bears. I'm not the scientist you need for this. I'll tell Comrade Brodyaga there's been a mistake.'

'Alyosha, you're an expert in genetics. Your heredity experiments attract much interest, and, if this army is to work, I need you and your brilliant mind.'

Undoubtedly, she is flattering him to stop him from making her life—and her work—more difficult. She is likely in the same position as him—can't refuse the project and wants to return to her own research quickly. Presumably, as soon as they prove this idea of a bear army is unworkable.

'I understand you, Anastasia Sergeevna. This is keeping you from your real work, as it is me.'

Something sparks in Anastasia's iron-grey eyes, and he knows he's said something wrong.

'No, you don't understand, Alexey', she replies tersely. 'This is my real work. This is my project, and I told them I need you to make it happen.'

Alexey reels. How could she need him? What could he contribute to this crazy project? As if reading his thoughts, Anastasia softens.

'We don't have time for patience, Alyosha. We don't have time to take it slowly. Bears live for many decades, and that is too long. We need to win this war sooner. Before the Americans attack us first.'

***

When Alexey arrives at the lab to start work the next day, Anastasia isn't there. An unseen official has put his research into boxes and moved them to his new laboratory, but a quick look in a few of the boxes confirms to Alexey the worst: they haven't kept them in any order.

The lab itself is almost so clean as to look untouched, and very carefully organised.

Alexey had hoped that today, everything would seem less preposterous, this idea of quickly breeding a bear army. But, no matter how he's turned it over in his head over the course of the week, it hasn't got any better. Can it be done? Perhaps.

'Who knows what work she's already done', Alexey comments out loud.

'I can tell you myself', Anastasia replies, briefly surprising him. 'I am sorry I lost my temper yesterday. I want us to work together on good terms.'

Alexey doesn't look up. Instead, he flicks through his research files, despairing over being able to find anything ever again.

'I have questions for you, Alexey', Anastasia begins after a moment.

'And I have questions, too', Alexey interrupts. 'I don't understand why an expert in crossbreeding would be interested in this. So far, you have said nothing about breeding bears with other animals. Unless you're interested in breeding bears with humans?'

'You're thinking of Comrade Brodyaga?' Anastasia replies, and laughs. 'It's true, he does resemble one. But, no, bears are smarter than Brodyaga. I want your help to make a better bear. A bigger, stronger, smarter bear. A fiercer bear. A bear that grows more quickly.'

'Anastasia Sergeevna, stop, please. This is too much all at once. What you're asking, maybe it could be done, but it would take many, many years of work. 100 years or more. Bears are not like fruit flies, unless we breed bears to have short lifespans.'

'Yes!' Anastasia replies. 'This is why I want you working on this. The bears can mature faster and live less long.'

'This is what I'm talking about; these things take time: a long time, and bears are complicated.'

Alexey's disbelief and outrage mix in equal parts with his exasperation that anyone thinks this is achievable and that he could be asked to do such things.

'We don't have time', Anastasia persists. 'We need to make this happen quickly.'

She is frustratingly serious, and little things like logic, or facts, or what is possible, won't matter to the higher-up officials.

Elsewhere, scientists are trying to communicate telepathically with animals, or move objects with their minds, or spy on their enemies as ghosts, or put rockets into space. What is or isn't possible matters less when there is a war to win and an aggressive enemy who might attack unprovoked at any time.

***

Months go by, winter becomes a frigid spring, and Alexey convinces Anastasia to talk a small amount of sense into the officials.

Can the bears mature faster? It can be done. Can they be bigger? At the expense of their lifespans. Can the bears be more aggressive? Alexey draws the line here. Bears are already unpredictable and more than capable of destroying a human with the barest effort. More aggressive bears will only end in the deaths of him and Anastasia.

The officials accept this; they can't afford to lose their scientists, so they agree that bears are probably aggressive enough.

Can the bears be more intelligent? Alexey explains, many times, intelligence isn't easily defined, and it isn't his area of expertise. Besides, do they want intelligent bears or subservient bears? Better to have an army that does what it's told, without question. He wonders if the officials would rather have a subservient scientist who does what he's told.

***

The experiments progress, and as Alexey marks three grim anniversaries since their work began, he tries detaching himself.

For his beloved fruit flies, their entire life cycle from egg to adult takes about 8 days, and he'd seen countless generations without giving them a moment's thought. You could never feel attached to a fly, but bears are different.

Visiting their cages and taking blood samples, Alexey is very aware of the sheer physical presence of the bears—they seem to take up more room than their bodies alone, and he feels a certain kinship when he looks in their eyes.

Alexey isn't one to imagine human traits in animals, nonetheless he now understands how some people think bears and humans are related.

Normally, bears could live maybe 25 years. Even with the lab's questionable procedures, experimental drugs, and selective breeding speeding their maturity, they still live too long. He and Anastasia are still euthanising too many bears and it wears him down.

When a line of experiments reaches a dead end, there still remains a seemingly limitless supply of bears.

He doesn't want to ask. With each generation of bears, Alexey feels part of his soul slipping away. He avoids seeing his reflection in the mornings, avoids making eye contact while he shaves and brushes his teeth.

A man of his age shouldn't be greying so fast; his hair had been lush and black before this work started. Is he also maturing faster, like the bears? Is his work shortening his own lifespan?

He tries bringing up the subject with Anastasia one day in the lab: could the experiments somehow be affecting him too? But she shrugs him off. She's not showing signs of greying or care. With each generation, she seems to burn with infernal fire.

***

In another lab, animals are quietly and selectively being bred for a different program. It's no secret that the USA wants to dominate space, and with it the USSR and the rest of the world.

USSR funds and attention are being diverted and directed towards the sky. They launch satellites in displays of supremacy over their North American rivals, followed by rockets. There are rumours of sending humans into space, rumours of plans to build a Moon colony. Yet still, Alexey's work continues.

His fears are soon confirmed, and animals start shooting into space. Alexey understands sacrifice, as everyone does. When he works late into the night, he does so because he knows all their sacrifices will be worth it, and he tells himself that generations of bears are also giving their sacrifice, just like the space dogs.

Noble Laika is the first, followed by Belka, and Strelka, then by Ham, Gagarin, and Tereshkova, and many others whose names are unknown and won't be remembered.

***

Everything is still a rush, still a race, and Alexey knows much is happening that isn't spoken about. The same as nobody knows about his experiments, Alexey is sure there are more sacrifices and journeys to space than anyone is admitting. It's better not to ask questions, unless you wish to find yourself an unwilling participant.

One ordinary grey day, following an unsuccessful night of trying to sleep, Alexey's hopes are sunk like a warship. In an unexpected visit, Saponya and Brodyaga tell the scientists that officials are satisfied with the progress they're making with the bears.

What Alexey thought would take hundreds of years is being achieved in a handful. Already their subjects are maturing in half the time and showing remarkable signs of intelligence. Anastasia's determination is paying off, as is Alexey's willingness to be led like a sacrificial goat. Recently, he's stopped shaving altogether, making it so much easier to avoid the accusing gaze in the mirror.

Brodyaga proudly announces that the bears, once trained, are going on a secret mission to the stars.

'What purpose does this serve?' Alexey almost demands from Anastasia after Brodyaga leaves them to their work; he knows better than to challenge an official.

'It makes no sense. We've sent humans into space, we've sent monkeys and dogs into space, and they survived. What purpose does it serve to send my bears?'

'Your bears, Alexey Pavlovich?' Anastasia asks. 'The bears do not belong to you. They're not your pets, your children. The bears are workers, the same as us.'

'Anastasia Sergeevna, I know this. But my question stands.'

'I know nothing more about this than you do. And it's not our role to know. We don't work with the space program, and we don't need to know.'

Of course Anastasia can't know any more than him, but sometimes he suspects she has more influence or power than he's led to believe. *Project Oruzhiye Medvedi* is her project, after all.

***

Alexey is dimly aware that, somewhere, his bears are being trained to fight. In some way or another.

Silently, he doubts that any amount of maturity or intelligence could teach bears to use weapons. Undoubtedly, they're large enough and strong enough to carry even a Degtyaryov-Shpagin Large-Calibre gun, but he can't imagine how they could fire it. Smaller weapons are easier to hold and carry, but a bear is not a man. It still makes no sense to him.

Alexey thought the invading bear army was to overwhelm the enemy with the number of bears, bears smart enough to attack the enemy instead of each other. He isn't consulted or involved in conversations about giving guns to an intelligent army of bears.

This isn't his problem, he tells himself. It is their right to arm bears.

But now. Now they talk about bears in rockets. Alexey admits transporting bears by rockets makes more sense than earlier plans to send them by submarine. He's unconvinced any bear could be intelligent enough to navigate a sub strategically, let alone several leading invading armies. Airborne would be better.

This is what concerns him. Planes and rockets don't need an ursine captain—they would have humans piloting them—but these bears could easily work parachutes. Advance infantry units of armed bears could parachute into several major cities.

The plan seems so obvious that he catches himself biting his fingernails. It's a dirty habit his father once had and something Alexey has always avoided, until now.

***

At first, Alexey wonders if the message he receives from Comrade Brodyaga might be a test. His conscience is clear, he's loyal to his work and to his country, and even if he sometimes vents frustrations to Anastasia, he doesn't see how anyone can suspect him of anything.

It's unwise, but Alexey knows he'll meet the official when he receives the message. He recognised something in the official's eyes the first time they met and now wonders if the man has hidden depths.

Meeting Brodyaga privately, Alexey is impressed. Not only are there not hidden depths, but what depths Brodyaga does have are surprisingly shallow. Instead, he has disturbing information: invasion plans are shelved while officials are working on something else.

Nobody is interested in an invasion any more, and fears of a first-strike nuclear attack are diminishing—with increasing numbers of satellites, it's becoming almost impossible for anyone to get the drop on the other, and all it could lead to is Mutually Assured Destruction.

What's more, some officials have raised the idea that an invading squadron of planes, each carrying an armed bear infantry, could be mistaken for such an attack. Nobody would wait to see what the planes are carrying.

Even if an invasion went ahead, Brodyaga says, there are questions about whether the bears will be loyal to their Mother Country. It's speculated that things could go wrong, and this bear army might breed with native North American bears. In that scenario, it could become a threat bigger even than the USA, and a controlling force in the world.

After all, the bears are weapon-trained and could access even more arms if their invasion were successful. Nothing would stop this bear army from pushing south through Central America and on to South America. An army of intelligent armed bears is considered too much of a risk.

Because of this risk, the plan to put bears into space isn't just one or two, Brodyaga shares, it's all of them. They are being sent to orbit the Sun, like Luna 1, where they will eventually burn up.

'I'm just a biologist', Alexey says. 'I don't have the influence or the access to the officials you do. Can't you just go through the proper channels?'

'There are no proper channels for stopping this', Brodyaga replies. 'These projects are so secret that barely anyone knows the bears exist. Scientists working on rockets know they're getting new volunteers, but it doesn't matter to them.'

Alexey sighs. 'What do you want from me? What do you want me to do?'

'You're smart, Alexey, and not just biology-smart. I'll put you in touch with another, and they'll tell you the plan. You'll work together for all the bears.'

'This doesn't make sense. I don't know why you need me.'

'An army of bears with machine guns makes no sense, but you didn't complain. You helped create them.'

Alexey feels a sting, whether the barb is intentional or not. Brodyaga has watched him pushing on with the army of the bears for years.

'You like the bears, same as I like the bears. There is a growing group of us', Brodyaga continues, oblivious as to Alexey's feelings. 'We can stop the destruction of all the bears together, Alexey.'

'And what about the invasion?'

'There is no invasion. We'll win because our ideology is pure, and capitalism will eat itself. Soon, capitalism will collapse, and Russia will have cities in space.'

With this talk of cities in space, Alexey thinks Brodyaga is clearly insane.

***

'We have a mutual friend.'

After five days of waiting for the contact Brodyaga promised, he'd begun to think it wasn't happening.

The voice on the telephone has a sing-song quality to their words, and Alexey thinks they sound familiar. If it's important to them that they remain unknown, Alexey doesn't care to find out who they are, but the tonality of their voice nags at him.

'That might be true,' Alexey replies, 'but I have told our friend I don't know how I can help you. I am—'

'You are just a biologist, I know. I've heard your objections. But I'm told you have one of the most brilliant minds in Russia, perhaps second only to your comrade Comrade Bratko.'

The use of Bratko's name is intriguing; not too many people know about their work together, and he knows better than to talk about it himself.

The caller continues: 'We have less than a week. You might be just a biologist, but we're counting on you, Comrade Tolubaev.'

'Counting on me to do what? This isn't a question of biology. I've no access or clearance. I don't even know what plan I'm meant to disrupt.'

'You'll receive a visitor. It'll become clear from then.'

As the line goes dead, Alexey's hopes of being left alone vanish.

***

The morning is bright but crisp, even in the shared laboratory, and Anastasia doesn't notice or care that Alexey is distracted.

She's gone back to formally calling him Alexey Pavlovich, perhaps out of annoyance, and he wonders if she realises how futile their work is and is mourning for what she's lost. Together they've produced the intelligent weaponised bears she devoted herself to, but for what?

Of course, Anastasia must believe they're performing some purpose—testing if their bears can survive the vacuum of space, lethal levels of cosmic radiation, starvation or dehydration. But surely she wonders why they would need intelligent, fighting bears when they could do the same with chimpanzees?

Several times, he starts a conversation with her, hoping to bring up the fate of the bears they've created together, but something always stops him. What did she say? The bears are not your children. On some level, they almost are.

He's never been interested in things like marriage or children; to each, he's always asked himself what purpose either served. Never having a satisfactory answer that seems logical, Alexey's few courtships always end in acrimony rather than matrimony. But, somehow, he now has an army of children and is in a kind of weird marriage with Anastasia, Brodyaga and Saponya.

A marriage he's about to destroy for the sake of his children. Not to mention, betray his country and risk death, or exile to Alma Ata, like Ivanov, 30 years ago.

***

Early in the afternoon, Anastasia leaves the lab early, without caring to tell Alexey where she's going. He supposes she's consulting on the Sputnik project that will doom her bears.

47

Someone must have known Anastasia was leaving, or were watching Alexey, because a visitor calls after he's alone. Wearing an ushanka hat and oversized coat, too large even for such a bleak winter's day, they seemed to be almost overcompensating as they attempt to disguise themselves.

'We are running out of time, Comrade Tolubaev', the stranger says brusquely without introduction, stepping in from the doorway of the lab.

Alexey can tell from their voice and stature that they aren't Brodyaga—though it wouldn't surprise him if the official thought he could be incognito, when anyone could recognise him in thick fog.

Although the visitor is keeping a careful distance between them, Alexey also notices now his guest's sing-song tone is as much of a disguise as their shapeless coat.

'I don't know what to tell you. Comrade Bratko is clearly working on the Sputnik project and doesn't know how it will end.'

'She must think there will only be one spacecraft', the visitor replies.

'There are many?'

'Of course, there are many.' The sudden coldness surprises Alexey. 'You can't put an entire army of bears into one spacecraft.'

'How many? Do they have enough for their plan to invade several cities?'

'Thankfully not. But there are to be three spacecrafts. We'll say they're communications satellites, and when contact is lost, we will blame system errors. Never workers.'

There is something familiar about his strange visitor. Alexey studies them as they speak and realises what it is. They have turned the collar up on their coat, not to protect against the biting wind, but to try and hide a small birthmark on their neck.

'I admit, I'm not a rocket scientist. But you, Anastasia Sergeevna, you must be working with others who also don't want this to end.'

Anastasia laughs humourlessly. 'I said you have a brilliant mind, Alyosha.'

'You try too hard to disguise yourself. And I didn't believe you could be ignorant or want this to happen.'

'There is someone. I don't know if we can trust him, but we don't have a lot of options. It doesn't matter to them where the spacecraft go, so long as they are lost …'

'I don't see what we can do, unless you plan for the spacecraft to not leave Earth at all?'

'No, that would be too risky. We can't afford the bears landing somewhere else.'

'Then what is your plan and where do I fit in?'

'That is enough for today, I first had to be sure we can trust you. Don't ask me any more questions.'

Alexey walks to the far side of the lab and stands by the window on the world. He hadn't noticed that while they had been talking, it had become dark outside. Preoccupied with his thoughts, Anastasia slips out unnoticed.

***

Alexey should have been troubled and distracted by what they'd set in motion, but instead, that night, he is quickly lost in dreams. In his sleep, he sees a spacecraft land alone in a dark forest, almost crashing in its steep descent.

Two cosmonauts—thankfully human—emerge from the damaged craft and into the snow. Before Alexey can see what's happened to the travellers, and if they will survive a winter's night in a forest, he's woken by a crash as the door to his apartment is kicked in. Someone has talked and implicated him in their scheme.

Alexey isn't given a chance to dress and isn't told what he's accused of. Hooded, Alexey is punched suddenly in the stomach, knocking the wind out of him, then sapped over the head before he can recover. Alexey is foggily aware of someone taking him taken away in a vehicle but doesn't care where he's going.

***

In a bare office, somewhere in a Moscow basement, Alexey is still groggy and struggles to tell how much time has passed since he was woken. Perhaps it's been an hour or longer, it could also have been much less.

Almost disconnected from himself, he feels like a scientist observing and noting his own directions.

Alexey feels the sensation of blood congealing on his head where he was struck, and the sticky rivulets that have run down his face, and he's aware at some point he vomited on himself. The combination makes him feel sick again.

Sitting across the desk is Saponya, his good humour from their first meeting nowhere to be seen.

'We know you're a traitor and a spy, Tolubaev. We know you've betrayed your country and your comrades. If you're lucky, we'll only exile you. But first, tell us who you're working with.'

Alexey is sure his exile will be by way of a bullet to the back of the head, whatever Saponya tells him.

'I'm not a spy. I'm not a traitor. You have it all wrong. I am just—'

'Just a biologist, Tolubaev? You scientists are like painters, you can't be trusted. We know your plans to sabotage the Sputnik launch.'

'You can't sabotage something that's planned to fail. What am I meant to be planning, making sure it doesn't go wrong?'

'The mission isn't your concern, Tolubaev. We're grateful to Comrade Bratko for keeping you under observation, and she's confirmed our suspicions.'

'Anastasia Sergeevna?'

'Comrade Bratko has been working with us from the beginning. You aren't so brilliant, Tolubaev; you believed what she wanted.'

Alexey's head is spinning, and he doesn't know if it's a concussion or the implication that nothing has been true. He's worked on this for years. He's personally seen the changes in generations of bears, generations genetically altered to mature much faster. If nothing was true, what was it all for?

Slowly, realisation dawns on him. He said it was impossible, and he was right. It doesn't matter how they deceived him; of course he was right. He almost feels like laughing. The idea of creating an army of fast-maturing intelligent bears and giving them guns. It's ridiculous. Why then does he now instead feel like crying?

'What happened to all the bears?'

'It doesn't matter. Did you think the bears were your children, Tolubaev? There are words for men like you, you know.'

Alexey wonders what people say about him behind his back when he works late into the evening and goes home alone to his apartment.

'Tell us who you're working with, Tolubaev, and you might live through this.'

Alexey clearly sees he's unlikely to live to see sunrise, and while the idiot Brodyaga's name comes into his head—a man too stupid to have been part of this trap—Alexey won't condemn anyone else to his fate.

Sensing Alexey's resolve, or just tired of the make-believe, Saponya pushes back from the table. 'Very well', he says, taking an old revolver from his belt, 'at least nobody will miss you'.

Alexey has sometimes wondered what he'd do in this situation. Would he attempt a dramatic escape while bruised and battered and tied to a chair? Would he sob and beg for mercy? Would he say something tough and look his killer in the eye before they pulled the trigger?

Instead, he looks at the floor. He feels disappointed more than anything. He's not scared but also doesn't feel brave. He almost wants Saponya to get it over with so he can get on with whatever happens to him next—or the absence of anything.

'I had to know we could trust you', Anastasia says.

Alexey looks up; he didn't hear her come in. Saponya is still holding his revolver, but he's no longer aiming it at Alexey, or at anyone. Saponya looks at Anastasia with a blank look that barely changes when she produces a semi-automatic pistol and shoots him. The gun makes little more than a pop sound. Saponya slumps to the ground.

'What's going on?' Alexey asks. He feels very far away and wonders if this might be a dream on the way to death.

'I'm getting you out of here, that's what's going on. I played along with them so I could be sure about you, but soon someone will find Saponya and notice you're not here.'

'Where are we going?'

'We're going to stop the bears being sent to their death. Where else would we be going?'

'I don't know. You still haven't told me what we're doing.'

Anastasia sighs and sits down, as if she hadn't wanted to get into this discussion after shooting a man.

'We've been changing their destination. If those in charge want the spacecraft to be unsuccessful, they won't be interested in checking details. For them, it only needs to leave Earth and escape our orbit. We're sending them to the Moon, instead.'

'That's the same as sending them to the Sun. They'll have no food, water, oxygen. Bratko, you're still condemning them.'

'I've been working with others for some time, Alexey. There is much you don't know. While the world thinks we're launching satellites, we've been launching other missions, using them as cover and a distraction.'

'For what purpose? We put the first satellite in orbit, the first humans in space, why would we keep this secret from the world?'

'There is a lunar base, a military and scientific outpost, hidden on the far side. We can destroy any unwanted visitors when they're out of sight of the Earth and keep our presence quiet. Here, we can preserve what could be lost on Earth, and, if necessary, we can launch a strike from the Moon.'

'We don't still plan a first-strike attack against the USA?'

'A first strike, no. But if they attack and disable our ability to respond, everything is lost. This is our last resort, they don't expect retaliation from the Moon, and our spies tell us the Americans won't make it to the Moon this decade.'

'And what of the bears? These spacecrafts can't fly themselves, and I hope the bears aren't so intelligent they can fly them?'

'Flying a spacecraft is not so hard, Tolubaev. Landing them is difficult. Given enough time and training, I think perhaps bears could fly them and maybe also one day land them. But I have pilots and we have now enough details and resources to launch this before anyone in charge realises where the spacecraft are going.'

'This is all real?' The details of the plan seem too elaborate to be anything he's dreaming, and that makes it even harder to accept.

'Of course it is. What's the matter with you? How hard did that idiot hit you?'

'Talking to Saponyo, an army of intelligent armed bears suddenly seemed … ridiculous. Impossible.'

'Well, it's all real, and if we don't get there soon, there are going to be a lot of dead bears.'

'I still don't understand where I fit into this. I think I understand your plan: bears go to your Moon base instead of dying in space. But why do you need me?'

'You understand these bears better than anyone, Alyosha. I've all your notes and observations, but you are the only one who really understands how much oxygen we will need, and how safely we can sedate them enough for the journey without knocking them out.'

Alexey feels a small glow, deep inside, realising his expertise is recognised, and that there is something he can do for his bears.

They have less than 48 hours before the launch, so he hurries after his rescuer into the Moscow pre-dawn. The biologist has a lot of work to do, and it will take them almost that long to get to the Baikonur Cosmodrome, if nobody finds Saponya first.

***

Before the citizens of Moscow can wake up, Anastasia drives them out of the city in a slightly battered black car. This Pobeda has seen better days, and Alexey presumes she's requisitioned or stolen the car. It's unremarkable enough to avoid attention.

The car's heater works, but barely, and its clock is decidedly stuck on 12:02, but despite his discomfort, Alexey falls asleep almost immediately in his bucket seat, grateful that Anastasia isn't driving a military vehicle instead.

He doesn't dream of cosmonauts in a forest this time but instead of Laika, alone in Sputnik 2.

Rescued from a life on the street, Laika became the first living creature to reach orbit and to die in space. In his dream, she's floating weightlessly in a small, cramped capsule, looking out the window at Earth.

He doesn't know how long he's been asleep when the car stops and Anastasia smacks him on the chest.

'Look alive, Alyosha. It's a checkpoint.'

'What are they checking for? Are they looking for me, for us?'

'I expect it's a random checkpoint. Don't say anything. Leave it all to me.'

'Whatever you say, Comrade Bratko.'

Anastasia shoots him a dark look before winding down her window where an official is waiting.

'ID, please.'

Handing over her papers, Anastasia announces herself: 'Bratko Anastasia Sergeevna. Going to Baikonur Cosmodrome on official business.'

'What is your business there, Bratko?'

'It's not your business to know.'

The soldier puffs out at being spoken to so abruptly, looking foolishly more like a dangerous fish.

Looking at her credentials, hoping for an excuse to pull rank, he instead deflates and silently acknowledges she's right. Glancing over his shoulder at his colleague who's speaking to a driver behind them, the guard relents.

It's too cold to delay this stop any longer, and he'll be in serious trouble if a complaint is made against him by someone as senior as Comrade Bratko.

'Very well, carry on, Comrade Bratko.'

Anastasia needs no further encouragement. She's deliberately slow winding the window back up before setting off. They can't be seen to be in a hurry to leave, or it will seem suspicious.

As their noisy black car pulls back onto the road, the official is walking towards them again.

'Stop!' he shouts. Anastasia ignores him.

'STOP! That is an order, or I will shoot.'

'Get down, Alexey', is all she says and accelerates hard.

The official shoots twice, and although both shots miss, Alexey presumes the man is probably trying to hit them.

'What was that?' he asks when they're far enough away.

'Could be anything. It could be they found Saponya, could be they've been told to watch for us, could be nothing. You know how it is.'

The next 20 to 30 hours pass without incident, giving Alexey time to work on his necessary calculations. Chewing the end of his now-blunt pencil, Alexey reflects how the only time he's been able to sleep recently is in a crisis, and he supposes he might feel more relaxed if the officer at the checkpoint had managed to hit one of them.

Occasionally, Anastasia lets Alexey drive. Even if it's only so she doesn't crash with tiredness, he feels grateful to be included and have something helpful to do.

Still unsure if he can trust this person, whoever Anastasia really is, Alexey considers she's saved his life twice today and it seems unlikely she'd go to that trouble only to double-cross him later.

***

The cosmodrome in Baikonur is less impressive than Alexey expected.

'It's mostly used for missile tests', Anastasia explains, unprompted.

But three spacecrafts are on the launchpads, fuelled. Alexey presumes their passengers are already on board the craft, though there is no way to see inside.

'What now?'

'Now we finish *Project Oruzhiye Medvedi*', Anastasia takes Alexey's notepad and calculations from him without thanks. 'Stay here, and don't get shot.'

Anastasia doesn't wait for Alexey to argue. While she's gone, he thinks he hears shouting and gunshots but can't be sure. He's fairly happy nobody is shooting at him.

Anastasia has been gone for precisely 37 minutes before she reappears. Alexey is aware how long she's been away because he has looked at his watch no fewer than 74 times to check it's still running.

Alexey recognises one of the men accompanying her. It could have been dense fog, and he'd still recognise Comrade Brodyaga. Anastasia introduces the other man as Serge Ivanovich.

'But where are the pilots?' Alexey asks.

'We are cosmonauts, Alexey', she says.

'We? But … I thought you were finding pilots. You're a pilot?'

'A woman can be a pilot and a scientist, you know. I joined the Air Force as part of the Cosmonaut Corps, and they commissioned me as an officer after my training. Then someone decided I was of better use elsewhere.' Anastasia almost shrugs.

Alexey feels like there's more to her story than she's sharing. She introduces the third cosmonaut as Comrade Koshmak.

'We haven't met, have we, Comrade Koshmak?'

'Met, no. But I've been following your work, and I agreed when Anastasia suggested we bring you into the project. Now we don't have much time, and it's important this mission is successful. The information you have provided us with will hopefully steer us right.'

'Goodbye, Alyosha', Anastasia says. 'In the car is a new identity for you. You can't go back to Moscow, but you have details of the people who'll help you.'

'Safe travels. Send me a postcard from the Moon.' Alexey is unsure what kind of goodbye fits a situation as surreal as this.

As the cosmonauts walk away, Brodyaga stops before striding back to Alexey, surprising him with a bear hug. Without saying anything, he walks away again, stepping out to catch up with the others.

'Don't wait for us, Alyosha', Anastasia calls over her shoulder. 'It's not safe. Don't worry, you won't miss the launch.'

Alexey does as he's told and doesn't wait to see the cosmonauts board their spacecrafts. Instead, he drives to the outskirts of a nearby town where he can be fairly sure nobody is looking for him.

On the passenger seat of the car sits an unmarked envelope, and all the necessary documents are inside: a passport, a birth certificate, relevant identity and work papers. There's also a handwritten page in Anastasia's writing.

She explains the backstory he needs to know for his identity, his contacts, and how they'll meet him at the Tyuratam station where he is to abandon the car.

The letter is as businesslike as Comrade Bratko is in person, and Alexey doesn't expect or receive any declarations of love or sentimentality from her.

Alexey stands beside Pobeda and waits. He thinks of the years he has spent working with Anastasia Bratko on this crazy project and the army of bears aboard the spacecraft.

Now a house painter named Oleg Makarovich Tereshchenko, he watches the spacecraft launch on their mission to the Moon.

The rockets are in the sky before he feels their sound in his feet—even before he hears it. As they disappear from view, the delayed sound of the launch still building, Alexey hopes his hurried calculations were correct.

Scared of Your Own Shadow

Looking back, he's always been there—behind me.

People joke about being scared of your shadow, like it's a silly thing to be scared of. But their shadow isn't a bear.

I'm not brave like a bear. I'm certainly not strong, and I'm not intimidating. I look in the mirror, studying my own features, right down to the tiniest patch of dry skin among the scattered freckles above my nose.

I search for some sign of bear, some ursa, either major or minor. But there's no great bear in my brown eyes.

My hands can't be described as paws by any stretch of the imagination; I'm not notably hairy and nobody would describe me as fierce. There is nothing in the least bear-like about me.

But on a sunny day, when I'm walking in the hills or jogging the path down by the river, that bear's shadow is forever a step behind me, dogging my heels and following my footsteps.

I know enough not to ask people if they can see the bear, but when I've asked if they ever think shadows look like other things they hesitate.

'Well, no', they say, 'What else could they look like?'

I tried, once, asking a friend if they ever think shadows look like animals.

'Like shadow puppets?' they replied. 'But do the shadows of animals even look like the animals?'

I didn't bring it up again.

Perhaps this shadow of a bear has eaten the shadow of me. Perhaps the bear will eat me next.

A Summer's Tale

In my memory, it was unusually hot that summer. Not just hot for England, but hot for anywhere. The kind of summer when every day there was a story about how Southend-on-Sea was hotter than the South Pacific or how Margate was hotter than Madrid.

I remember the newspaper office equally clearly, like one of the artist John Baeder's photorealistic paintings. If you asked me to, right now, I could draw for you its 1970s décor and brown carpets, and you wouldn't be able to tell if the windows were tinted or if they never got washed. There was no air conditioning, and there was a room where people went to smoke. People snapped at each other all week long.

Barry, the Post's sub-editor, smelled like stale sweat. He'd lean over me to read the copy on my computer screen, and the smell was like a mix of dried vinegar and mouldy potatoes. I doubted almost everything I wrote for him.

Sometimes, I sat dejected on the concrete out back and gave myself a pep talk. Even now, the smell of rubbish bins on hot days makes me a little nostalgic, like that one song that sounds like it could only have come from August 2009.

Other than the weather, there was nothing much to talk about: rubbish collectors still striking; England fail to qualify; trains delayed.

The bear story was a weird one, though. Especially weird: we were an Essex newspaper; the bear was 90 kilometres away in Ipswich. But I guess it made a change from writing about how Little Baddow was hotter than Barbados.

Bear roaming Rendlesham Forest. Multiple eyewitnesses. YouTube videos. Warnings from authorities.

I heard about it, and I saw my future. Brave junior reporter covers story, finds local angle. Front page news. National papers run our story because it's better than anything they can do.

I may as well have imagined sub-editor Barry carrying me on his shoulders in front of a cheering office. Most of the time, he only spoke to me to ask me to make him another cup of tea.

But no, Jeffrey, Echo crime reporter, was the one who went to Ipswich. It wasn't a crime to be a bear, but we didn't have a reporter for bears.

'This better not be about a teddy bear's fucking picnic', Jeffrey said to no one in particular. It was like he wanted it officially on the record. He spent too much time in courtrooms.

I laughed, and he glared. I felt a twinge of guilt, worried he thought maybe I had made the story up.

All afternoon, Barry kept making the same joke about Jeffrey going on a bear hunt. Nobody was listening, nobody laughed, but he kept on at it, laughing like a drain.

Thanks to Jeffrey, I had an ice cream van in my head, driving round and round and round, endlessly playing the same off-key tune. If you go down to the woods today, you're in for a big surprise.

I kept catching myself humming the song absent-mindedly. Every time I stopped, and every time I'd start again a few minutes later. Part of me worried Jeffrey would be hurt, and I felt bad for laughing about the teddy bear's picnic.

He won't be hurt, I told myself, sitting in my spot of concrete in the shade by the overflowing bins. I left for the evening before he came back.

The story ran on page five in the morning edition, under a story about a plane enthusiast's obsession with Concorde. My piece about an elderly couple's wedding anniversary made page eight. They didn't include my byline.

That night, someone in the online comments for Jeffrey's article about the bear hunt said the forest was haunted. Haunted by a group of bear miners who had all their gear stolen. Today's the day the teddy bears had their picks nicked, the commenter said.

I hoped Jeffrey wouldn't see the comment, or he might think it was me. Anonymous others chimed in with theories, ideas, conspiracies of their own. Some with tales of strange sightings in the forest, but mostly just picnic jokes.

***

Jeffrey was in court the next day, some private school suing a tree surgeon over their Dutch elms. Barry must have called him about the bear hunt.

It was a hoax.

The whole thing was set up by a theatre troupe promoting their production of Shakespeare's Winter's Tale, a play remarkable only for the stage direction exit pursued by a bear. I was relieved. I'd never heard of it.

I mentally checked the other points from the list I'd made at 3 am the night before, staring at the ceiling and worrying that Jeffrey would think I had something to do with the whole thing.

I'd never been to the forest, let alone unconsciously joined a theatre group 90 kilometres from home who performed in the woods. I didn't even own a car. I didn't inexplicably try and write stories about bears. I couldn't have had anything to do with it.

Stranger In My Skin

'*There is a considerable overlap between the intelligence of the smartest bears and the dumbest tourists.*' – **Yosemite park ranger on why it's hard to design a bear-proof garbage can** .

The first time I woke up knowing I was a man, I felt like a stranger in my own skin. If you don't know what I mean, I envy you.

I wasn't sure if I'd been sleeping for days, but I was unbearably hungry, and everything felt quiet and far away. It was very wrong.

When I opened my eyes, the fading daylight was familiar, my surroundings unchanged, and I was relieved. Before I realised that everything else felt out of focus—the smells, the sounds, the colours. It was all washed out.

The night before I could have told you about 500 different scents: a bear that had walked through recently and was now a mile away, humans cooking food nearby, or a dozen different berries I know by their smell alone. But now I could smell damp earth and rain. Little else.

Then I noticed the obvious: my hands. More specifically, I had hands. Human hands. Startled, I tried to get up—but collapsed quickly. I had other parts, between my legs, things I didn't even know humans had. It didn't seem very useful.

I wondered what breed of human I was. Do humans even have breeds? You come in different sizes and shades and shapes; some are clearly small—cub-like, loud, and shouting but harmless, some grown, still loud and shouting, but angry and not harmless. Overall, there are no real clues for a bear like me to go on.

Now here I was, a human. All I knew was that I was hungry, naked, and vulnerable, and I had to move. Most important was doing something about this insistent growling in my stomach—but I'd no idea how humans hunt for food.

I know humans kill. I've seen humans shoot deer and rabbits, and I've seen them shoot bears who were no threat to them, but I've never seen them eat what they kill. Often, they take it with them, presumably back to a den, but I don't know. Their food comes in packets and metal containers.

I might not have been able to smell food or see well in the rapidly fading light, but I knew where to find it without going too near the humans. I went where they threw the food away, near the canvas enclosures they sleep in.

As a bear these containers had eluded me. They smell so enticing, but it's like they have been designed to keep me out. I can bite them, stand on them, turn them over, and still get nothing. Luckily, most of the time, humans overfill these cans so much they won't shut. As a human ... I thought it would be easier to open.

I knew pulling on it wouldn't work, so I explored what other features it had. Once I found there was a small opening to put human fingers into, it took a little work, but I did it. Fingers seem very small and fragile, so it stands to reason they have some use like this.

What smells appealing to a bear now made me violently ill. Half-eaten lumps of meat, rotting fruit, bones. Eating the can's bounty of discarded food with my bare hands turned my stomach with a violent lurch, like an animal in distress.

Then there I was: naked, cold, throwing up for the first time in my life. I also felt something new: afraid. I didn't know what was happening, and I was scared that I wouldn't survive it.

It's wrong to say I'd never been afraid before—I've been threatened, I've been hunted by humans, and I've run for my life from grown bears before I was old enough to know why.

But I've never worried about the future before. Not that I could articulate any of that, not at the time. Or used words like *articulate*.

A pair of humans came from somewhere, startling me and scaring them. They stopped abruptly, looked at me like they thought I was a bear. The irony. Then their relief that I was a human turned to horror when they saw I was a naked human, kneeling on all fours, retching in the grass.

One of them made that noise humans make when you surprise them as a bear or meet almost literally anything that isn't a human, or sometimes another human. You know the sound I mean? High pitched. Hurts your ears. Hurts my head.

A scream? Yeah, that's it. I still forget words sometimes. Not so articulate, I guess.

They screamed. I stood up to be my fiercest and realised I wasn't that fierce at all. I did what sometimes I have to do: I ran.

Humans can't run worth shit. Sometimes when I've chased them, they've given it a try. Have I ever killed a human? Let's not talk about that. Right then, I couldn't run worth shit anyway. I wasn't used to having only two legs. On top of that, I was hungry, and I had no idea where I was going.

I don't think they chased me. Imagine, being chased by a human! I ventured into the safety of the woods in search of food, before remembering the obvious: there are bears in the woods by this camp and the lake. Instead of finding something I could catch and eat, there was more chance of being killed and eaten myself. What did that leave? The usual. Berries, grass, insects.

***

The rest of the night I avoided humans, staying around parts of the edges of the camp where nobody was staying, and where there was no food for humans or bears. I could barely stomach any of the berries or grass I tried to eat—and ants bite, too; nobody ever tells you that. Humans get tired quickly, especially when they don't eat. No wonder they don't hibernate; they wouldn't survive. That and they'd get eaten by their stupid dogs.

No. Don't get me started on dogs.

What? No, I've never spoken to a dog. I'm not a dog. Bears don't even talk to each other. I can't describe it.

I fell asleep eventually. Cold, naked, huddled in the hollow of a log. I wished I could smell the stories on the log—usually, I'd be able to read them all: who else had passed by, and when. I'd know when I was last there. Tonight, it smelt of damp moss and nothing more.

***

I awoke once, briefly. I don't know how long had passed; time is something I can't get the hang of. We don't do time. Not how you do. Bears eat. Sleep. Hunt. There's no five minutes, two months, 10 years. It was around dawn when I fell asleep, and some sudden noise disturbed my sleep later—but whoever or whatever it was, I fell back into a dark well of sleep quickly and was grateful for it.

The next thing I knew, it was getting dark, and immediately I realised I was a bear. Everything was alive, and everything felt quieter. I wasn't glad to be a bear any more than I was worried about the future. I just was.

No, I don't have a bear name. I already told you, bears don't talk. We don't need language because the world doesn't exist in words.

***

I don't know how long it was before this bear was a man again. I recognised the feeling before I opened my eyes. My thoughts were racing, and I knew that I was changed and the danger I was in.

My memories of the last time being human were fuzzy, but I could feel my way through them. One thing I rarely felt as a bear was cold, so I had to do something about that.

I didn't know if this change would keep happening, how long it would last, or if I'd ever change back. I couldn't go around uncovered.

Bears know where we can find what we need, and there's so much that humans keep in their canvas enclosures. Mostly food. At least, bears have little interest in anything else inside them—including the humans. But the idea came to me that humans must keep their body coverings—their clothes— n these places, too, since you rarely saw uncovered humans.

As quietly and slowly as I could, I walked on my spindly human legs in the direction of the human canvas enclosures. The daylight was disappearing quickly, and I was struggling to see clearly—this also meant humans might be close, too, lighting fires to cook their food.

I was lucky. When I got to the enclosures, everything was quiet. While I couldn't hear or smell if the humans were nearby, I was sure there'd be more signs of them if any were around, and it was too early for them to be sleeping.

About to make a run over to one of the enclosures, I heard a sound. My heart started racing and my thoughts all came in a tumble like rabbits—and the comparison to rabbits made me hungrier, even while everything was screaming danger. I don't get how humans can live like that.

A deer ran through the clearing, and I hoped it wasn't scared by a human with a gun.

I didn't want to spend another night unprotected, or be caught naked again, so I took a chance. Running over to one of the canvas enclosures, I realised I didn't know how to open one.

Unlike the discarded food cans, this isn't something you worry about as a bear: the canvas parts easily with paws, but human hands won't tear or shred anything.

I briefly attempted using my teeth, but a human mouth and teeth are frustratingly small. They're worse than hands. But I remembered hands are good for something: using a tool. I fumbled around until I found a sharp rock.

The canvas had something resembling an opening, but I didn't know where to start. The little metal things clearly did something, but I relied on my bare instincts instead—if this was meant to open, it would tear more easily if I used this rock like a large claw. I was right, too.

Once inside, I looked around and grabbed whatever I could. I was pleased to be figuring things out, learning things, but I also knew that stopping here promised danger.

What? Of course, I took it! I didn't know or care about things like sizes or anything else in human minds. You think you know where this is going? Maybe you do.

Where was I? *Clothes?* That's what they're called, right. Clothes. And tents? There you go. Clothes are fabric coverings, and tents are canvas enclosures. Got it.

I didn't know what I needed or how much I needed, but I knew I'd need something for my feet and something to cover my body. Nothing seemed to be in any order or have any indication if it was necessary. From somewhere outside the tent, I heard human vehicles' noises, so I snatched what I could and ran back to the woods.

Looking at what I'd gathered, I could tell the foot coverings—no, don't bother, I don't need to know all these words, you have too many words—weren't the same, but they appeared to be the same kind of size.

The clothes were enough for whatever they were. I looked them all over for a little while before working out how this thing was meant to go. My bear memories weren't clear then, more like pictures, but I tried to visualise how I'd seen it worn: with the head going through a hole at the top, and arms through smaller ones on the sides.

Nothing felt right. I took a long time getting the foot coverings on, and, even then, they were painful. It explains why humans are bad-tempered and angry all the time if these things hurt so much. Clothes were better; at least wearing them wasn't painful, but this thing wouldn't keep me very warm since it hardly covered my legs.

The important thing was at least now I'd look the same as any other human. It would make finding food easier for me if I wasn't worried about being uncovered. As a human, it seems like a lot of time is spent worrying. I remembered from last time I was in this shape that eating what humans throw away is a bad idea. I know that berries and grubs and grass aren't a good time for humans, either. I was sure I wasn't going to try ants again.

I didn't know what that left.

Then I had an idea: in some places where humans throw away food, they must have it another way. Fresh. I would go there, just like a normal human, and I would eat my food like a normal human, completely identical to every other human. You all seem very similar to me, so I thought this would be simple.

Even as a human, I could smell food and make out some sounds. So I walked in that direction—one human foot after another.

***

I eventually found the building. While we're on the subject, why don't humans use these buildings all the time instead of those canvas enclosure tents? Never mind. I can tell from your face the answer wouldn't make sense.

There were other humans around, so I tried to act like one of them. As if I was just a normal human. Not a bear in some hopefully temporary human form, nor a bear with barely any experience of being human.

As I walked in through the doors, I caught the humans sitting and standing inside noticing me, though none of them seemed distinctive. My mind was chattering again, full of noise. Full of fear.

Do humans smell fear? They could tell something was different about me, and I wished I was a bear. Then we would see who was afraid. One of them shouted something I didn't understand. Humans shout a lot.

I didn't know if he was shouting at me, but I considered turning on him. Of course, I didn't. I knew I needed to be more human and react less.

Inside, the building was noisy and bright and full of people and the smell of cooking food. The smell of meat grilling and sizzling was dizzying. Some humans stopped and looked at me, but they quickly lost interest.

'What do you want?' a human asked me. Several humans were sitting and leaning against that large barrier they call a bar, with their food on top of it, too.

I'd never had to speak to a human before, but understanding them didn't surprise me. I was slightly surprised I could speak like a human, but you humans seem simple creatures, so it would make sense.

'Umm ... food?' I replied.

'OK ... so what do you want to eat?'

'Other than food?'

'Yes, other than food?'

'Do you have ... meat?' I was worried they might try and give me something in a metal container.

'Best barbecue in the state!'

'That's meat?'

'Of course it's meat! We aren't vegans!'

I didn't know what those were, but the human was friendly, so I went along with it, copying their behaviour and their volume and their face's expressions.

'Yes, I'm a human, too,' I laughed.

'I know what you mean, son.'

I must have said the right thing.

'How do you want your steak?'

'My ... Steak?' I didn't know what steak was. I hoped it was an animal.

'Your meat.'

'Yes! Right! Food. Meat. Steak.'

'You want it burnt or bloody?'

'Burnt ... or bloody?' I've said before, humans have too many words.

'Do you want it well done or rare?'

'Or bear? I'm not a bear. I'm a human! Look at me, I'm not covered in hair! I'm wearing clothes! I'm walking on two legs!' My voice was rising. They could somehow tell I was a bear, and I was starting to panic. If they shot bears, I didn't know what they'd do to a bear that looked like a human.

'RARE. I said, rare!' The human almost shouted above the noise.

'Rare is definitely how I want to eat my steak', I agreed, quickly. 'Could I ... have that ...' I carefully felt my way through words as if I was following a trail. I wanted to leave this place already.

'Take out?'

'Yes. Take out.'

'I guess so, but it's going to get cold before you get back to your trailer.'

'Right. My ... trailer. Yes.' They didn't seem to notice my hesitation.

'You sure you wouldn't rather have it here, friend? Good company, good people.'

I declined.

Then they wanted me to pay. This isn't something I'd seen humans doing, but I was lucky. Although I had no idea what they meant, I'd seen other humans produce objects from their clothes and give them over before they were given food.

Perhaps things were hidden on me, too, so I looked. And there was something like this thing, your wallet.

I pretended to be normal and handed it over. The human gave me a puzzled look, but they took things from the wallet and returned it.

Soon they gave me food in some kind of thin cardboard box; I could feel the heat through the sides starting to burn my soft human hands, but I took it eagerly. Then, for a moment, I paused.

I'd started by copying the human to look more normal, but the more we'd interacted, the more I felt like I genuinely liked the human. Distracted by this and whether to leave, I didn't notice two humans were giving me more attention than the others.

As I was making my way out, back into the night, one of them pointed to me—the physically smaller of the two humans —and said, 'I think that's my dress'.

The larger human stood and they could almost have been a bear, not unlike yourself. Before he could take a step towards me, the other human stood— and I knew this wasn't as simple as territory between bears. I'd violated some human rule and was unclear what would happen next.

'Hold up there, fella; I need to talk with you', the smaller human who had pointed me out was walking defiantly towards me, and she didn't seem friendly. So I ran.

I'd expect humans to have better legs for the amount of running you seem to need to do, but I was into the night and into the woods, and apparently, she didn't want to chase me. I didn't know what was going on, but she clearly didn't like my clothes.

In the dark, I found my way to a familiar lake, deep in the woods, and greedily ate my steak with my hands. I was sick of my human clothes already, so before I walked into the cold, still water, I took them off and immediately felt freer.

At first, it was peaceful, being alone in the cold water of the lake, until I heard human voices. I could do nothing from where I was, and as a small group of humans appeared, I hoped they wouldn't see me.

'Someone else is here', one of the humans said, finding my discarded clothes.

'I don't know', another human offered, 'these clothes just look like junk. The shoes don't even match, and this dress has been half ripped'.

'Maybe they belong to that guy?' a third human said, catching sight of me trying to remain motionless in the lake.

'Did you lose some clothes here, hoss?' the human who'd said my clothes were junk called out. There was something in their voice I didn't like.

'Maybe he's who stole the things from Mike and Julie's tent.'

The second human was quieter, smaller. I was noticing the little differences between some humans. Perhaps they were slightly similar bears? I had a vague shadow of a memory, of how some humans had different smells to them.

I decided not to answer the humans. Maybe if I kept quiet, they'd go away? Humans often tried that with me, acting like they weren't there, backing away slowly.

The humans said other quiet things to each other that I couldn't hear, then I saw them taking the clothes from where I'd left them by the lake.

Without warning, the first human picked up a rock and threw it into the water near me. They shouted angrily, more noise than words, and then the other humans followed, picking up stones and throwing them into the lake.

Moving about in water was more difficult than running as a human, and their aim was improving. One rock painfully struck my shoulder, and I roared.

The humans only laughed and threw more. The next hit me just above my left eye, and immediately I felt blood running down my head, and everything started spinning. I don't know whether this was what the humans wanted, but they stopped throwing the rocks and ran away from the lake, still with my clothes.

They hadn't been mine for long, but still, I was angry the humans were taking them away from me.

The human group gone, I swam to the edge of the lake and rested. I didn't know what to do now. I don't remember clearly much of what followed except that I stumbled onto another group of tents a short while later.

Humans were sitting in chairs around a fire. I briefly surprised them, but the sight of me naked and bleeding must have reassured them I wasn't a threat.

They wrapped me in a warm, itchy, blanket and asked me what happened. I explained the story to them as best as possible, with what words I had and the pain in my head.

I'd been swimming, people took my clothes and threw rocks at me. I didn't say anything about where the clothes came from, or the human earlier in the night who had said something about her dress.

One human cleaned the wound and bandaged my head, and when they had finished, the group gave me clothes and had me sit with them by their fire. These clothes suited my body better, they covered it more fully, and I looked more like the hairier humans.

This was good. I'd begun to feel if I was to imitate a human better, it might keep me safe if I looked like most of them did. The ones who covered their legs in the rough clothing I wore now, instead of the flimsy and smaller clothes I ripped trying to wear.

As one of the humans was showing me my bandaged head in a mirror, for the first time I saw my reflection. I felt like an outsider looking at myself, recognising I was me, this human, with rust-coloured rough hair on their face and green eyes.

'Want a drink?' one of the more ragged humans asked.

'I'm not sure that's a great idea, Grant. Our friend here's injured and maybe shouldn't drink on top of that.'

'Let him answer for himself, Denise', the Grant human replied, then, more softly, 'He might appreciate it'.

'I agree, a drink.' Being agreeable is important, and I *was* thirsty, now that they had mentioned it. I hadn't known I could get anything like that along with the food earlier, though lots of the humans in the bar had drinks. I also wasn't sure now about the water I'd swallowed at the lake, but that could have been the head wound.

'Want a beer?' the human who had been given the name Grant asked me.

'A bear?' Why was Grant asking me if I wanted a bear?

'Easy there, big guy, I said beer. You're a might easily startled. Do you want beer, to drink? Maybe you're right, Denise.'

'Oh, yes … I was making a joke. Yes, beer.' I tried to say the word the same way as Grant, and the humans looked at each other, but they didn't object and gave me a cold metal can.

I drank from it the same way as the humans. It had a taste almost like overripe fruit does, and I remembered one summer how that had made me feel. But beer was mostly like cold water, and that was good enough for me.

'Where you from, hon? You're not from around here.' This was the human called Denise.

'You'd be surprised', I almost laughed.

'What do you mean?'

'Nothing. I feel like I'm from far away.'

'Like Montana?'

'Yes, Montana is where I'm from.'

'That explains why you don't understand beer!'

All the humans in the group laughed at this. Grant and Denise, and even the other two pairs of humans that were uninterested in us stopped talking to each other and laughed. I wasn't sure if they were laughing at me or laughing at Denise.

Part of me felt strange they were laughing at Denise. She'd helped me, and I liked her for that.

'Montana folk are weird', Denise said. 'My eldest left Wyoming with a girl from Montana. That girl has a be-hind like a waterbed's been shoved down the back of a pair of Levi's. She's a nice girl, right though, always sends me a Christmas card, which is more than you can say for my no-good ex.'

I didn't understand any of this. But I agreed; it was easier. I didn't know what Montana meant or what Wyoming was, but it was worth trying to remember. Places don't need names. There isn't a spot where once place ends and another begins; there isn't a line where my territory ends.

'… Never understood what Natalie sees in her …' Denise was still talking, seemingly to herself since Grant appeared to have lost interest. Perhaps he already knew this.

'I need to leave', I said, attempting to stand up.

'Do you need to go far?' Grant asked. 'I'd offer to give you a ride, but I'm in no state for driving.'

'I'm sure I can find my den from here.'

'If you're sure?' Denise started, but I insisted.

'Do you want these back?' I started taking off the clothes.

'No!' their combined shout startled me.

'Why don't you just stay the night here?' Denise asked, and I got the feeling it wasn't a question. 'We've got an air bed that will do you, if you don't mind sleeping under the stars out here.'

I could tell it would be easier to just go with what they said, and they gave me another one of their beers. Maybe this was what human life was like: agreeing to things sometimes even if you didn't want to.

'Beers not bears', I said, mostly to myself, as I accepted the bottle from Grant, practicing how the words sounded.

'I'll drink to that', he agreed.

That's all I remember of the rest of that night. When all the humans had left me alone, I removed the clothes, pulled the blanket on top of me, and I slept.

As I fell asleep, I half expected to be woken up by Grant the next morning and still be human. I was half right.

The shouting and commotion would have been impossible for anyone to sleep through. I know this reaction—usually it comes when looking for food around humans. Screaming, shouting, panic, and someone inevitably grabbing a gun. I didn't need to rely on my bear instincts to know to get out of there.

***

I visited various camps again several times as a human before I met the same group of humans. I wasn't sure I'd remember them. I didn't know if they'd remember me.

How do humans remember each other when your eyesight is bad and you can't tell anyone apart by how they smell?

At least I knew when I met other groups of humans they weren't the same ones: they treated me like anyone else, with the same kind of distance and slight distrust; nobody called me 'Montana', and I could feel they weren't the right humans either.

Once or twice a group would offer me a beer and to join them. Almost inevitably their conversations involved talk of hunting, and I had to leave before anyone mentioned bears. I'm sure people started remembering me.

I got better at finding clothes, and not wearing the clothes in the same places I found them. I learnt how to wear clothes like a human, at least clothes that fitted me—I still don't understand why you enforce some clothes for males or females. Or why females can wear clothes like males and not the other way around.

I know that wearing clothes isn't a choice, you don't have to be so defensive. But if you were covered in fur you wouldn't need to wear fabric clothes, and since you do so well in other areas, your lack of fur seems like an oversight. But what was I saying?

I learnt to blend in better. I learnt to stop jumping if I thought someone said 'bear'—and learnt that nobody knew I was an impostor human.

That was about the time I met Denise and Grant again. I thought they'd be surprised to see me, but at the very least they were smiling and laughing.

'Well, shit, it's *Montana*!' Grant said. 'We all thought you got killed by a bear. Want a beer, son?' He was pulling one out of some ice water and opening it before I could reply.

'Where you been, Montana?' Denise asked, with a quiet, distant sound to her voice.

That was difficult to answer. 'Just ... around.'

'Around here?' Denise had something on her mind.

'I've been around. That's it.'

Grant had a twinkle in his eye as he started to interrupt, before one of the other humans spoke up.

'Shush, Grant, let Montana speak', they told him, and I began getting an odd tingle down my spine.

If I was a bear, I'd have had more information to work with. I'd have been able to tell from the scents on the air if there was danger, or prey, or what people were feeling.

These transformations hadn't been once or twice, they were a regular thing. How often? I don't know. We've already talked about time; time for a bear is different. I don't know how much time passes.

And, yes, since you ask, I *can't* read. You seem surprised. Why would I read? Bears don't read, why would we? But I speak English? Is that what you call this, *English*? Then I guess so.

I don't know *how* any more than you do. I don't know why I am human at some times and a bear at others. I've heard humans speak all my life; you talk too much and have too many words. I pick stuff up.

I've heard radio and television. Yes, I know what a radio is. No, I don't know how to work one. They seem like unnecessary noise. I don't know what your words mean when I'm a bear, but I pick up what I need to, without needing a language.

I notice the seasons change, as a bear and human. I notice people get older or things are different. I notice that I change, as a bear and human. I notice the hair on my face changes colour.

But the more times I change, however many times there have been, I notice a different change: the outline between a bear and human is becoming less distinct.

I feel a bear inside of me as human, and even feel some human inside me when I'm a bear. It's like remembering the outline of a dream.

I wonder sometimes, when I'm human—what if I'm *not* turning from a bear into human and human into a bear. What if each time I'm leaving something behind? And I wonder what will be left.

OK. Yes. Denise, Grant and friends.

'Do you have a real name, Montana?' Denise asked.

At that moment I started to worry—worrying about things is really something I don't miss when I'm a bear—talking to strangers that I don't see again isn't the same as talking to these people, the closest thing I had to friends. Or family, for that matter.

'Not really?' I didn't look at her, I didn't want to make eye contact. But I could tell how she was looking at me.

'How can you not really have a real name? Everyone has a name. Even Gopher, here—don't you, Gopher?' Grant gestured towards their friend who'd *shushed* him.

He looked uncomfortable. 'You're the only ones who still call me that', he started. It seemed like he was going to say something else, but then not-Gopher just shrugged and silently went back to his beer. I like humans that talk less.

'I'll tell you a secret, though, Montana', Grant continued, his voice now a mock-whisper, 'he's not a real gopher'.

'But I am a real doctor', not-Gopher said with a smile, making Denise and Grant both laugh solidly.

'Why is it funny that you're a doctor? A real doctor? Not a … pretend doctor?'

It was absurd anyone would mistake a human for a gopher. But what about doctors?

'It's a long story', not-Gopher said, 'besides I think I'm really more of an otter'.

Not-Gopher smiled to himself. This was more confusing than talking about doctors. Gopher was a human and no more an otter than he was a gopher. Or a bear.

Denise turned back to me suddenly. 'What did your parents call you, Montana? Are they still alive out there, living in … Montana?'

'I didn't know them. I sometimes remember my mother, but it's more like … shadows. They're not clear.'

'Childhood memories are like shadows', not-Gopher said slowly, nodding to himself. 'I like that one. You're real smart, Montana.'

'You're an orphan, hon?' Denise asked.

'Aren't we all?'

Young humans grow so slowly and spend much time with parent-humans. I remembered being chased away by my mother when I was still very young, and I was surprised by the memory.

'I hardly remember my mother, and I don't have siblings. I guess I had to grow up fast. I think that's normal.'

'I don't much remember my mama either', not-Gopher agreed. 'When I was ten, my mama, she got real sick and my sister and me, we had to go stay with my uncle Ted. He always made us go out when he had "company". That's what he called it, having *company*. He meant *ladies*, but he said it like it made him fancy.'

Everyone had grown quiet while not-Gopher was talking, and Denise looked at him gently. 'You've not told us about that before, Ben.'

'Where did you go that day, Montana?' Grant asked me suddenly, and the mood was broken.

'What day? I go to lots of places. I go to the bar, or I go—'

'You know what day', Denise had a new flintiness to her voice.

'Almost exactly two years ago. We always come back here to camp around the same time. You were hurt, we helped you out, gave you some clothes. You remember.' Grant had also lost some of his sparkle.

'There was a bear in the camp, and Grant chased it out. Woulda shot it if he could. But there was no you, Montana. You left without saying goodbye.'

'There was a bear, I was scared, so I left.'

'You left without your clothes? And you didn't come back later? We stayed around for days. Didn't see that bear again, lucky for him. Didn't see you neither. The ranger said he didn't reckon you got killed by the bear, or we'd have likely found *something* left of you.'

'Lots of people knew you, but none of them knew your name, or where you're from. Said they saw you alone at the bar or saw you swimming. Some said they thought you was a thief, but nobody had proof.'

I could smell it. I wasn't sure at first, thought it was my imagination. Humans can't smell like a bear can. But the more they talked, the stronger it got. They were afraid of me.

What should have been a thrill and excitement of anyone fearing me was instead something like fear of my own.

If they were afraid of me, then they knew I wasn't like them.

'You ain't really from Montana at all, are you?' Grant asked.

I stood up. I knew I wasn't big like a bear or strong like a bear. I wasn't even particularly tall for a human. But I wasn't going to be afraid.

Something in them recognised I was more than just an average height, shabbily dressed, human with no name or family.

While their beer made my head spin a little, I'd had similar experiences as a bear. I liked it then and didn't dislike it now.

'I could tell you a lot about who I am.' I said, and in that moment, I could remember almost a lifetime as a bear.

'I can tell you about climbing, I can tell you about tearing into trees with claws and teeth, I can tell you about how the night feels and how the world smells, I can—'

'You could have told us the truth when you met us', Denise said, softly. She still smelt afraid, but I knew she liked me, and I don't know why but she trusted me.

'Told you what? That I don't know who I am? That I don't know *what* I am?'

'You're a human-bear. Or a bear-human', Grant said.

'A what?'

'Either you're a human that turns into a bear, or a bear that turns into a human', Denise said. 'People have told stories for thousands of years about men like you—'

'Stop.' I said, quietly. I didn't need to raise my voice or intimidate them. I could just be.

'I'm not half anything. I'm not a human that turns into a bear. I am a bear. Sometimes I'm a man. But I'm still a bear.'

'My cousin dated a man whose grandad turned into a bear', Denise said. 'She didn't see it happen with her own eyes or nothing, but she believed the stories. They weren't imaginative enough to make it up. You could have told us.'

Right then, I understood Denise. I understood why they'd been afraid, too. It wasn't they were afraid of a bear; they were afraid of the man who kept secrets and didn't trust them. They'd helped me when I was hurt.

And I understood why humans do so well even if you can't run, can't see in the dark, can't smell anything, and eat things from metal containers. Some humans will just accept you for yourself. Sometimes they look past appearances and see who you are.

Where Are We Going?

When the first scientists announce a revolutionary technology allowing animals to speak, pet owners are delighted.

Imagine: your beloved Buster expressing devotion. Soon, surrendered companions fill the shelters. Pets—through no fault of their own—were often less articulate than hoped.

Animals aren't unintelligent; they simply don't need to express themselves for humans to understand. Humans translating animal sounds into speech doesn't change that.

Some animals are better suited to it than others. Guinea pigs are dreamy and thoughtful, often slightly abstract. Tortoises? Surprisingly oafish. You can't talk to cats.

Zoos become problematic. More problematic, perhaps. You can't keep wild animals in substandard enclosures anymore—the animals have something to say about it.

***

13 August. With an open mind, I open the door to the cage. And out he steps.

I'd thought zoos, and places like this, would have heightened security, with so many people collaborating with the animals to let them out. But it's a quiet day, rainy and cold, and almost nobody is around.

I was honestly surprised people were paying me no attention, too busy huddling into coats and looking for hot drinks.

The rain makes everything feel alive, and beyond the petrichor every enclosure is now fleshed out with millions of different smells—from bedding to undergrowth to food and waste. The bear's enclosure has a heady, musty smell from his damp fur.

We stand in silence for what feels like a century, inspecting each other. I don't know if I'm supposed to avoid eye contact; it seems futile: there's nothing to stop him opening up my torso with the absolute barest of effort.

As I look into his dark eyes, he stares back into mine. I feel like there's a question on his mind, but he doesn't speak. I turn my back, begin to walk away. He follows me, my lumbering shadow.

We pass toddlers dressed as Tigger with balloons tied to their wrists, and retired couples in matching Burberry raincoats and scarves. Some shyly sneak a second look at the pair of us.

Nobody says a thing.

If there's any thought that we're unusual, the bear and me, people don't care enough to ask.

Approaching the turnstiles, my heart begins thumping. Sure I'll be stopped, or questioned; I play it cool, smile and say thanks to the zoo kiosk attendant.

Looking up from her dog-eared copy of *Into the Wild* the teenager appears puzzled, rather than alarmed, that I'm walking out in the company of a bear. But she says nothing.

We step into the street, and I look up and down, trying to remember where I left my car.

'Where are we going?'

The bear's voice is deep, as soft and rich as his fur. I'd expected it to be gravelly, perhaps faintly accented, but instead he sounds only weary.

***

The bear and I are living together for several months before the dreams start.

People ask if I'm seeing anyone, and I make excuses, say something about my flatmate, the bear.

Sometimes they're confused. You can hear the cranial cogs turning as they try to find a connection between the words *flatmate* and *bear*. Sometimes a smug smile spreads across their face.

'A bear', they say, smirking. 'Bears, hey?'

'Not that kind of bear,'

'Oh, but I didn't mean—'

'I know what you meant, and that doesn't automatically mean bears.'

'I wasn't trying to—' they attempt to extricate and excuse themselves before realising it's worse if they meant it literally.

It's worse implying *I'm in a relationship* with the bear.

People once claimed allowing same-sex marriage would lead to folks marrying pets. If you can imagine something so daft, some strange minds really thought it likely. And you know it didn't. Talking to animals didn't do it, either.

You could barely even say we're friends, the bear and me. We live together, and the bear is free to leave. He doesn't need to give notice.

***

'Where are we going?'

He leans forwards in his seat. I turn down the music, and he repeats the question: *Where are we going?*

I tell him.

'Of course, of course', the bear says, remembering, embarrassed to have asked again.

Back up goes the volume and he's gazing out of the window at the scenery rolling by. I guess he's never really been anywhere other than the zoo.

Indian Ocean Drive starts in Perth and ends a dusty 400 kilometres later in Geraldton. The bear certainly hasn't taken any road trips, so I'm secretly snatching glances at him as the scenery changes. Going from the other-worldly desert landscape of the Pinnacles and Nambung National Park to the white sand dunes of Lancelin, to the turquoise waters of Jurien Bay, and pushing on to Geraldton.

Indian Ocean is usually slightly quicker than other routes, but even if it isn't I prefer it for seeing the ocean.

Connecting various coastal towns directly to Perth, the road's been positive for many of them—though the impact of the global financial crisis is still visible, along with the years without international tourists coming to stay. Stopping places overnight, the bear and I sometimes wander the streets to get a feel for it.

There's an eerie atmosphere to the faded billboards still advertising land for sale in abandoned housing developments. Fancy mansions are islands, their balconies overlooking deserted streets.

***

The bear has been having dreams of falling stars, and the northern lights making a sound like music. He's never even seen the northern lights. I found him a book of nature photos to confirm we're talking about the same thing.

Were his dreams normal? It's becoming hard to know what normal means. What's normal when animals talk and a bear is your flatmate?

What concerns the bear about his dreams is that, until recently, he doesn't recall having any dreams before.

We rule out neurological causes, thanks to a discrete friend at a private hospital. Nobody else is reporting such dreams, so that also discounts side effects of the animal speech technology.

There is one scientist in the whole country who listens to my story and discusses it with bear at great length. That's why we're on this trip. I'm surprised that the scientist is in Geraldton, but he says he's connected to the museum.

After taking a scenic route and several days to get there, bear has another surprise for me, and the scientist.

He doesn't want the dreams to stop.

Three Simple Things for a Successful Zombie Apocalypse

'There's three things you need for a zombie apocalypse.'

Daisy thinks it sounds like a YouTube video tutorial: *top three things for starting a successful zombie apocalypse*. She presumes Jeff means three things for surviving, rather than starting one, and waits expectantly.

Jeff first drains his glass, not noticing the amber drops of cloudy IPA clinging to his reddish beard. His brow furrows, and his grey eyes get serious, so Daisy doesn't point it out.

'The first', he announces, 'is axes. Forget crossbows, they're fiddly and, sure, they might be silent, but they're as difficult to get hold of as a gun'.

'Isn't it unwise to throw away your weapon?'

'That depends. You don't always have to throw it. If you're faced with just one zombie, then throwing an axe is a safe bet. They're kind of just lumbering along, so you can hit them from a distance.' Jeff pauses, reflecting, and picks up his glass. He looks briefly surprised it's already empty but presses on.

'If you don't get the head, you'll still do some damage, and retrieving a thrown axe is easier than a crossbow bolt. But you're right.'

Studying the pint glass in his large hand for a moment, Jeff seems to be considering it for both distance and velocity against a slow-moving, relentless enemy. Then he discards the idea and with it the empty glass.

'Maybe it is better not to throw it. With a decent-sized axe, you can still get a-swing-and-a-hit without being in biting range', Jeff ponders, briefly agreeing with himself with a nod.

'But if you can throw it with accuracy and retrieve it without putting yourself at risk, that's best of all–'

Jeff mimes throwing a large axe with two hands, starting from behind his head, and Daisy wonders where and when and why he learnt how to throw an axe.

'Failing that, a good swing at their face, and it's job done. If you miss the face, you're probably going to hit the neck and take the head off.'

Jeff is holding court, as Daisy's Mum calls it. Is it *holding court* or *holding forth*? Suddenly she can't remember. Holding court sounds reasonable. A king sits on his throne, demanding everyone in his court listens to him. But holding forth also makes sense.

Maybe both are right? Daisy's hand twitches as if to reach for her phone, but she resists Googling it.

For a moment, Jeff seems like he isn't going to continue, and Daisy worries he's annoyed she interrupted. It's not that she especially wants to discuss zombies, but she also doesn't want Jeff sore at her.

Daisy looks at her uncle indulgently, hoping he'll continue his how-to guide for the end of the world.

'Climbing: that's your second most important thing', Jeff announces. 'Zombies can't climb. Traditional zombies, I mean. *Night of the Living Dead*, "when hell is full the dead will walk the Earth" type zombies. Not your *28 Days Later* fast zombies. Besides, they're a metaphor-'

'What for?'

'What?'

'You said the zombies are a metaphor. I'm not disagreeing; I don't know what they're a metaphor for.'

'Rage, it's as if the virus is man's inhumanity to man. The virus is literally called rage, but it doesn't matter, anyway. They aren't dead, so they aren't really zombies.'

'Strangely, that all makes sense', Daisy admits with a smile. She'd expected a lot of nonsense, but his points seem logical so far.

Imagining Uncle Jeff in his rock climbing shoes, small colourful Velcro shoes that remind her of the black plimsolls she wore in primary school, Daisy hides a grin behind her beer glass.

Would Jeff's zombie survival bag include these shoes? And does he plan to seek refuge in a local climbing gym should an undead horde advance on North Perth?

Maybe he plans to grab a couple of boxes of pizza shapes, a handful of giant pythons, a Gatorade, then climb to the top of a wall, hang out and wait for everything to blow over.

Daisy's amusement quickly fades. When the global pandemic got too close for comfort, and businesses closed, and everyone stayed home, Daisy had still believed the whole thing would blow over quickly.

She hadn't doubted the existence or seriousness of the virus; she just inexplicably thought that 'society' would defeat it quickly and easily. Maybe she'd been led astray by zombie movies where they wrapped everything up within a day or two, in-universe. But, back in reality, she's learnt it's unwise to underestimate these things. Two years on, very little has blown over.

'Wanna know the third thing?' Jeff is sitting down with a couple of fresh pints for them both. He visited the bar and she barely noticed.

Glad of the prompt out of rumination, Daisy lifts her head.

'Can I try and guess?' she asks. Jeff had been starting to get loud, even against the volume of the space. He was fully into the swing of his how-to guide stuff, and this could be an opportunity to take things down a notch.

Jeff looks surprised.

'No, really. I bet I can guess.' Daisy pauses for a minute, making a face like she's thinking, as if she's choosing from a whole list of possible options—rather than trying to think of one.

'A bike', she says, defiantly. 'A bicycle, not a motorbike, obviously. That needs fuel, and it's noisy. But a bicycle can be fast, it's nearly silent, it keeps you fit, and you can replace one pretty easily.'

'It's a great suggestion, Daze', Jeff replies, pensively scratching his head. There's a 'but' coming; Daisy can hear it.

'*But* Daze, a bicycle isn't as effective as you think. Yes, it's quiet and surprisingly quick, but you risk accidents and injury.'

After a few drinks, Jeff always starts using Daisy's childhood nickname, Daze. It's clumsy, but it's her uncle's awkward way of showing affection.

Hang on to the people you love, Daisy thinks, and recognises she's dangerously close to further craft beer-fuelled rumination.

The last 36 months have been rough and considering how those in charge are running the world she isn't filled with optimism for the future.

Daisy starts to ponder her uncle's motivation for inviting her out tonight to his favourite *warehouse-turned-microbrewery-and-pizzeria*, other than that he's a sucker for 90s industrial nostalgia.

The tables are barely more than long planks of wood across industrial barrels; though the air ducts are exposed, they're suspiciously shiny, and the walls are bare brick. Daisy thinks how the place must have cost a fortune to set up, and in five years it will feel uncomfortably dated.

The overhanging industrial lights stir lazily in the air currents, and Daisy's dark fringe casts ominous shadows over her eyes and face.

'Walking is better than cycling, truth be told', Jeff is still talking, not noticing his niece's drifting thoughts.

'Yes, it's slower, but there's no risk of falling off and hurting yourself. And walking is even quieter than cycling. Better yet, it's easier to stop. Plus, if you walk everywhere, you keep fit so you can easily run when you need to.'

'That's it? Your three things for the zombie apocalypse are rock climbing, axe throwing and walking? That last one is a bit of an anti-climax, to be honest, Uncle Jeff.'

A chef is singing in the open kitchen, and a 20-something is celebrating winning a game of shuffleboard in the back corner. Jeff raises his voice again to be heard better in the pizza warehouse hubbub.

'Come on, Daze, just call me "Jeff". You make me feel old, with your Millennial shite and your TikTok and calling me *Uncle Jeff.*'

A couple a short distance away stop talking for a moment and cast a worried glance at Jeff. The woman is dressed up for the night. Her sleek brown hair all but shouts how long she spent straightening it, her vintage prairie dress is crumpled enough to be expensive, and her silver shoes could outshine the Full Moon.

In contrast, her companion looks like he lives in one pair of jeans, and he might have washed his football shirt, but its crumpled look says *I found this on the floor then put it on.* He probably owns a multi-purpose marketing agency.

The mismatched couple's matching glance suggests they think Jeff is angry and are probably debating if they should post in their local Facebook community group.

Daisy thinks perhaps, on some level, Jeff is angry. She supposes her uncle is mad at the inevitability of getting older and how stupid it is to be mad at getting old precisely because it's inevitable, and maybe he's quietly angry at his inability to effect meaningful change on the world. But he's certainly not mad at her.

'You're changing the subject!' Daisy insists, 'I don't talk about TikTok, and I'm not even a Millennial. You're trying to distract me from how your zombie apocalypse tutorial is bullshit because it includes walking!'

'I'm not!' Another glance from the couple and Jeff lowers his voice a notch. 'I'm not changing anything. And it doesn't. I didn't bring up walking, you did. Wait, no, you brought up cycling; I said walking is better than cycling. But you wanted to guess, and I let you, and I haven't even got to the best bit yet.'

'OK. We'll agree to disagree. Please, if you will, continue.'

'Good. Because it's bears.'

'Bears?'

'Bears.'

'Bears as in ... bears?'

'Bears as in bears.'

Daisy is no clearer if 'bears as in bears' means the same thing to Jeff as it does to her.

Does 'bears as in bears' mean Fat Bear Week, the *Baron of Beardonkadonk*, 'I know I'll die trying to pet this' bears, or does 'bears as in bears' mean large, hairy men who like other men? Bears, perhaps, as in Uncle Jeff.

'Why bears?'

Why not? They're big, they're strong, you can befriend bears with careful feeding, and from then on, they'll tear apart anyone that threatens you—zombie or otherwise.'

Jeff's explanation resolves nothing. They still could be talking about either bear—and it's life-or-death to know the right kind. Offering raw steak to an enormous grizzly could get her killed if her uncle means you should be friends with, and feed, kind, large men.

It occurs to Daisy there aren't bears in Australia—and her monkey mind wanders off, wondering about what would happen if you introduced breeding pairs ... before she quickly stops it, catching herself.

Since there are no bears of the four-legged, shaggy-fur, cute-ears, enormous-jaws kind, maybe Jeff does mean bearded men in flannel shirts who can't get work as lumberjacks, so they brew their own ginger beer instead.

'To recap, the three things you need for a zombie apocalypse are axes, rock climbing skills and ... friendship with a bear?' Daisy is unsure she has this right.

'I don't know if you can call it *friendship*, exactly. Friendship requires sharing, trust, common interests. In a zombie apocalypse, you have a common interest in survival, but you're putting yourself first.'

'Adjust your own oxygen mask before assisting others', Daisy nods to herself.

'Exactly. It's not a lack of compassion, either look after yourself first or you can't help anyone else.'

'What's your point, you can't be friends with a bear?' Daisy looks quizzically at Jeff over the rim of her glass, still unsure what bears they mean.

'No, not at all', Jeff replies, defensively. Daisy wonders if it's because they're talking about humans after all, because she misunderstands his point, or because she misjudges platonic human-animal relationships.

'What are you getting at, then? I don't think a bear would eat a zombie, for the record.'

'I didn't say a bear would eat one. Only that bears will defend themselves—and you at the same time—from a zombie threat.'

Daisy nods enthusiastically and takes a large, thoughtful gulp of beer. She didn't ask how strong it was when she ordered it at the start of the night, and now she considers if that's something else to get some clarity on.

Jeff visibly relaxes. His whole demeanour lightens, and his shoulders drop as he takes the opportunity to drain his glass. It's a warm night, and he drinks quickly at the best of times. Especially when he's talking, and he's at least one beer ahead of Daisy.

But whether the bears in question are human or animal, Daisy feels safe around her uncle because she knows he'd do anything to protect her—the same as she would for him.

'I tell you what though, Daze: I'd be glad to have you with me in a zombie apocalypse.'

'Where did that come from? Because I drink pints?'

When Daisy first came home from uni, her parents were shocked at her unladylike drinking habits. Some people still are, and she gets prickly.

'No, I mean ... remember that punk band you were in? Unless I'm mistaken, you're the same Daisy Carter that stopped playing in the middle of a set to punch a guy in the crowd.'

'Yeah, well. He was harassing someone. They were in trouble, I jumped in ... and I got a black eye for my trouble. So, what? You want me around because I'm a tough chick? Anyway, that was 20 years ago...'

'And now I feel old again. Thanks for that.'

Daisy shrugs. 'My folks tried forbidding me from gigging after that, but I think they knew there was no stopping me.'

'There it is, that's the point I'm trying to make—there was no way to stop you, either from gigging or from helping people. I was proud of you, you know. I pretended to disapprove in front of your mum and dad, but I admired you. I honestly don't know if I have your bravery, then or now.'

Daisy realises things have become quiet. The chef has stopped singing, and the shuffleboard players have shuffled off to another venue.

'But anyway, friendship?' Daisy's voice is like a placid lake.

'Yes, friendship. You don't make real friends in a zombie apocalypse because it's not a priority. But a bear would have your back.'

'Where does this leave our three things?' It's getting late, and Daisy is aware that while nobody is asking them to leave, employees have started cleaning around them.

To her, the pizzeria feels more like an old warehouse now, and all this talk of apocalypse has her on edge. She hasn't felt truly relaxed in far too long.

'Yes. The three things you need for a zombie apocalypse', Jeff picks up their dropped thread. 'You need to be able to climb to escape, you need axes to defend yourself, and you need a bear on your side.'

'Bears as in bears.'

'Yes, bears as in bears', Jeff repeats, looking slightly puzzled.

That settled, Daisy pulls her phone out of her pocket and opens YouTube. 'There's a video I want to show you of a bear called Jimbo.'

'Is this from what you're always sharing on Facebook? I don't understand most of what you share on there.'

'What, *Wild Green Memes*?' Daisy asks slowly. 'No, that's not a YouTube channel, funnily enough it's a Facebook group', she explains, 'and I need to adjust my privacy settings if you can see those things'.

'I won't tell your mum.'

'About bears?' Daisy asks.

'No, that you're ... you know.'

'What? I mean, no. It's fine. You can just say *queer*. But sometimes I think Mum knew before I did.'

Briefly flustered at the conversation's abrupt turn, Daisy swears her burning cheeks must be glowing in the dim light. While she doesn't hide these things, she also doesn't talk about them with family.

'So, the video?' Jeff asks. Daisy is keenly aware that he knows he's steered them on an errant course and now he's trying to get back to safer waters.

'Doesn't matter, moment's gone.' Daisy laughs, more to herself than anyone. Suddenly it does seem funny. The whole night seems funny, getting pissed with her uncle over pizza, talking zombies and bears.

Then, just as suddenly, Daisy feels as if she's high above the Earth, looking at everything going on below. As the feeling of distance passes, a wave of gratitude washes over her. She's thankful for the here and now, for family and friends, and pizza, and beer, and bears, and the relative safety of her sleepy little west coast home.

'You alright, Daze? You looked a little space cadet for a second', Jeff asks, with paternal concern in his voice.

'Yeah, I'm fine. I think the beer's kicked in, is all. Lucky for me, I don't have work in the morning.'

'It's why we call you Daze. You've always been a daydreamer.'

Daisy laughs, and a waiter wiping tables looks up in surprise.

'I'm not the one planning how to survive a zombie apocalypse with only the aid of my rock climbing shoes, some bears, and a chopper!'

Jeff starts replying, then frowns. Daisy turns in the direction he's looking and sees a man has walked in wearing motorcycle leathers, complete with a helmet and its visor down. It's late to be collecting takeaway orders.

Jeff mutters something underneath his breath, but before Daisy can ask him to repeat it, there's pandemonium from the front counter.

The arrival isn't a food delivery driver, Daisy realises, because they're now pointing a shotgun at an employee shouting about the safe.

'Don't do a thing, Daisy', Jeff's voice carries a steely note of caution, but she doesn't need telling. She isn't getting anyone killed by trying to act the hero.

'They can't see us over here', she whispers back, her mind racing. They can call OOO, but by the time the cops arrive, the robber will be long gone.

'Are you fucking deaf?' he shouts. 'I want everything you've got in the safe.'

'I can't open it now', the employee stutters out. 'Not even the owner can.'

Daisy's attention divides between the robber at the counter and her uncle across from her. He warned her not to do anything, but there's no telling what he might do. She reaches across and squeezes his hand.

'Unc—I mean, *Jeff*. Please.'

'It's OK. I'm not', Jeff whispers back. 'As if I stand a chance anyway. What am I going to do, throw a pizza dish at the guy? It's not like I have an axe.'

'If only he were a zombie', Daisy stifles a giggle,, scared of attracting unwanted attention.

Meanwhile, the robber apparently isn't giving up easily. 'You think I'm stupid?' he demands. Answering his question would be dangerous.

'Really, it has a time delay', the employee is close to begging. 'Please, we've cashed out, and the safe won't open until the security company arrives tomorrow.'

Thrown by this turn of events, the robber appears torn between arguing or making a run for it. Perhaps he's weighing up the benefits of pushing it further, against how believable the explanation is. He must know that the longer he sticks around, the greater his chance of getting caught. Then again, if he runs, it was all for nothing.

A split-second decision made; the robber hits the employee in the face and runs for the door.

Outside, a motorbike roars to life, the sound already fading into the distance as Daisy and Jeff look at each other, shaken.

Daisy makes her way cautiously to the front counter where the employee slumps bleeding, and three other employees resurface from hiding places, on guard for anyone lying in wait.

The injured man has blood all over his face, but he's alert and doesn't seem too badly hurt. The name embroidered on his shirt says he's Andy, but the pizzeria's shirts probably come with generic names already stitched on them.

'Help's coming, Andy', Daisy reassures him. 'You did a great job, even if it's never worth risking your life for something like this. You did good.'

'I wasn't trying to!' He practically sobs the words. 'It's true, we can't open the safe. There's even a sign on the front door, next to the QR code.' Andy seems to be edging into anger.

'It's OK, mate', Daisy soothes, keeping Andy from hysteria. 'We've called an ambulance to get you checked out, and if the cops arrive first, they can ride with us.'

Jeff is talking to the other employees, though Daisy can't hear what he's saying from where she's sat on the floor. She isn't due in work at the hospital for another three days, but now she'll be there sooner.

She knows the response to expect when she comes in with Andy: *Bloody hell, Daze, what've you done to this guy?*

'Hey, Andy', Daisy starts. She's got a good idea for keeping him calm and lucid until help arrives. 'Do you know what three things you need for a zombie apocalypse?'

The Hitchhiker

It makes sense that a great burly black bear is in the backseat of the car, snoring.

Picture your average, typical car: this is it. It feels completely unreal because nothing is ever so normal as this. So, of course there is a bear asleep in the back.

'That's *Bear*', the driver says, as you climb into the passenger seat and start to buckle up.

He says it like maybe you've never seen a bear before. But he also says *bear* like it's a name. Not *a* bear, or *my* bear, or *the bear that was stolen from the zoo three days ago in a daring daylight robbery*. Just … Bear.

'Is he OK?'

'*She's* had a big day', the driver replies.

'Right, of course', you say, correcting yourself. 'But is she ok?'

Meanwhile the ursinologist in your head is screaming about the elephant in the room. Or the bear in the car.

'She'll be right .'

The driver has the radio up, and the hosts are chatting about last night's episode of The Bachelor. It's like they're oblivious that you're sharing a car journey with a bear-thief and their bear.

You've had awkward rides, hitchhiking on Indian Ocean Drive.

Heading out of Jurien Bay, you once spent 25 minutes while a guy mansplained to you how sea lions aren't really lions and aren't really seals. You didn't mention your marine biology degree. This ride to Perth feels comparatively sane in comparison.

As the driver starts singing along to some pub rock classic, you smile to yourself. Bear is stretched across the back seat, the afternoon sunlight through the half-open window makes her lush fur shine with rainbows, her chest softly rising and falling with each breath.

The Storytelling Hat

'Nobody ever handed me nothing', Lyndsay's grandpa tells her on her eleventh birthday.

Even at 11, the irony of this doesn't escape her. It's her birthday and he is literally giving her a present.

'I've worked for everything I ever got. I don't expect things to be handed to me like magic tricks because I'm—'

'That's enough, Grandpa', Lyndsay's Dad cuts him off, laughing, but with the familiar worried look he sometimes wears around the man.

'Quite capable of achieving on my own', Grandpa finishes defiantly, with his signature scowl. 'Happy birthday', he says, handing Lyndsay a battered top hat.

Lyndsay thinks this is possibly the least joy anyone has ever put into the word happy, like when she had to say 'sorry' to Travis in Mrs Drury's class the week before. She wasn't sorry for hitting him when he called her stupid, and her grandpa isn't happy.

'Thank you, Grandpa!' Lyndsay exclaims.

Always a polite child, Lyndsay learnt early how to fake gratitude for eager relatives giving well-meaning but unwanted presents. Her wholesome enthusiasm for her Grandpa's gift, however, is wholly genuine.

The Storytelling Hat. Correction: Grandpa's Storytelling Hat is perhaps the greatest gift anyone could offer, including a real unicorn. Maybe not the unicorn, but anything else.

With unabandoned joy, Lyndsay is quickly wrapping the still-scowling man in a surprisingly strong hug before he has time to think of excuses to leave.

At that moment, you might even have seen a flicker of warmth on Grandpa's grisly face, but only if you can also catch a hummingbird on the wing.

Lyndsay wears the hat for the rest of the day. Many of the various aunts, uncles, and family friends who pass through the smart Greenwich townhouse are confused and disappointed when their gifts are almost ignored in favour of an old hat. Just the same, nobody denies how the hat goes surprisingly well with Lyndsay's sparkly purple dress, smart black blazer and red high-top shoes.

When concerned relatives ask the uncharacteristically quiet girl if she's OK, Lyndsay looks surprised to see them for a moment, as if she's forgotten who they are or where she is. Then, she immediately brightens and explains. She's thinking about a story.

Tommy, Lyndsay's older brother, feels ignored by his sister for the first time in his life. It's as if a sun that once shone on only him has disappeared behind a cloud. And he doesn't like it.

No stories get told that day.

***

Despite being an increasingly grumpy old man, when Grandpa is unravelling a dramatic yarn, his troubles seem to disappear from his body. The world falls away for both the storyteller and his eager audience.

Grandpa doesn't tell stories without the hat, and Lyndsay remembers him explaining in hushed tones how it was a magic storytelling hat. The stories came from out of the hat, he said, and he told them.

Lyndsay is unsure if magic exists, though she saw a magician at her friend Suzie's birthday party, a kindly, Italian-accented man with green eyes that sparkled, He was quick with a joke, but Lyndsay wasn't convinced by his tricks, even if she couldn't tell how they were achieved.

Magic or not, she thinks, there must be more to the hat than just being *old*.

***

Lyndsay's Storytelling Hat, handed to her by her grandpa, was once handed to him by his own granddad.

Grandpa said it has been in the family for centuries. Given the hat's condition, Lyndsay's Dad once briefly questioned this, and quickly learnt not to: the Storytelling Hat was a story in itself, and it didn't matter if the story was true, embellished or entirely fictional. Some of the best stories are a mixture of all three.

Lyndsay's grandpa has enjoyed his reputation as a master storyteller. When the man put on his Storytelling Hat, he would spin dramatic tales of love and loss, life and death, adventure, and humour—no two stories were ever the same. Even if you wanted to hear a story a second time, locations and events would change, and its heroes could become the villains.

When you asked grandpa to tell a story about his own life, the results varied. Caught in the right mood, he'd dust off his Storytelling Hat, and a colourful thread of story would unfurl for eager listeners. But after grandpa lost his wife, he started spending less time with people and more with talk radio. He also became less likely to put on his Storytelling Hat.

Still, the adults closest to him know the topics to avoid or safe subjects to expand on. There remains a warm, kind man inside of him, and when he's in the right mood, a gentle, playful soul shines out.

***

Once, Grandpa was always making time for sharing stories with his children, and then his grandchildren, but he had become increasingly bitter, envious, and paranoid. Now, he was quietly angry at the one thing he expected the least: getting old.

A little under a year earlier, during the Christmas school holidays, Lyndsay and Tommy visited their grandpa at his house in Dagenham, not far from where the royal docks give way to East London airport.

Lyndsay's parents dropped off the children at his house in the morning, but the siblings quickly grew bored and restless when grandpa wanted only to watch football in peace and wouldn't tell them any stories. That's when and that's why they wandered off together to explore his house.

Lyndsay always felt slightly afraid of the master bedroom in her grandpa's house. The curtains were always closed, and even when you turned the light on in the room, it didn't get much brighter.

As far as she knew, her grandpa slept in a single bed in the sparse, undecorated spare room, so Lyndsay didn't know why there was a large double bed in the master bedroom.

She guessed the imposing dark wardrobe contained all his clothes, even though he didn't wear a wide variety of shirts or pants. Behind the closet was a large, shadowy crawl space.

The dingy space felt almost impenetrable. Lyndsay didn't know what might live there and did her best to stop herself imagining the monstrous possibilities.

On this day, boredom got the better of the two of them, and they ventured into the room. After a short while of playing there, they got used to the musty smell and the dim light—though they didn't think to open the curtains and let in the daylight.

Lyndsay and Tommy sat on the bedroom floor playing the latest inscrutable card game Tommy had learnt at school, but when Lyndsay got bored of Tommy's shifting rules, they inevitably wound up squabbling more than playing.

That's when Lyndsay had the idea of playing dress-up.

Putting out of her head any thought of disturbing whatever lived behind the wardrobe, she slowly opened the large wooden doors, climbed inside and pulled the doors shut.

Lyndsay was quickly disappointed, though wearily unsurprised: Grandpa's wardrobe wasn't a portal to a magical world of talking bears and the northern lights. So far, no wardrobe ever had been.

What the old wardrobe did contain was a treasure trove of old clothes and hats that she pulled out onto the floor of the bedroom for the two of them try on.

Tommy wore grandpa's sports coats and suit jackets, swamping the small-framed boy in tweed and polyester, and Lyndsay tried walking in her grandpa's shoes, clomping about the bedroom, trying not to trip over her own feet.

Then she found his hats—a dusty straw hat riddled with holes, a moth-eaten flat cap, and ... his Storytelling Hat.

Lyndsay fell quiet when she saw it.

It felt wrong to her that the hat still existed when Grandpa wasn't wearing it. It was almost a part of him, or like he conjured it from thin air when he wanted it, vanishing it when he didn't.

A thin silver chain adorned the sturdy felt of the hat, and a shiny peacock feather stuck upright in the hatband. Holding it in her hands for the first time, the hat felt no less magical to Lyndsay than the times her grandpa wore it to tell his stories.

Tommy had always been an anxious boy, and now there was a rabbit running laps in his stomach. He'd never liked the room and could hardly be encouraged to go in there at all most times, though he'd never admit to it. Judging by the activity in his stomach, he felt like they were doing something very wrong when his sister put the hat on with a flourish.

'I am the great storyteller!' she announced in a voice like a circus ringmaster.

Tommy had absolutely no idea why his sister used that stupid voice, but he was unimpressed. Grandpa didn't put on any theatrics when he wore it.

For her part, Lyndsay expected more from the hat. Grandpa's stories were animated, elaborate, fascinating; so the young girl hoped that she'd somehow transform when she wore the hat. Disappointed, she felt no change at all.

Just the same, she continued her performance: 'I bring you stories from centuries gone by', she exclaimed. 'Stories of monsters and mice, stories of heroes and horses. You will gasp, and you will cry!'

When Lyndsay was four or five, Tommy spent several months in hospital and Lyndsay could tell her parents were worried about him.

From that young age, she took it upon herself to try and distract the family with her exuberance. Sometimes now she couldn't tell where the act ended.

In her mind, Lyndsay was now standing in a circus big top, dazzled by the lights, and she was too alive to the rapt silence of the crowd—of which Tommy was at the centre—to hear the footsteps on the stairs.

Neither of them noticed when the man appeared in the doorway.

'Just what the bloody hell do you two think you are doing?' Grandpa roared like a bear, and both children jumped.

For once, Lyndsay was at a loss for words.

'Do you behave like this at home? Do you? Do you pull all your mum and dad's things out onto the floor, like a couple of filthy pigs?'

Tommy felt his anxiety rising like water about to overflow an unattended bathtub. The creepy room, going through grandpa's belongings without permission, and the surprisingly angry old man was all too much.

'Who said you could come in here?' Grandpa continued, before he turned his focus to Lyndsay.

'You, at least, should know better! The pair of you have all the brains of a clockwork mouse between you. Now, get out of my sight.'

Although Lyndsay was 24 months younger than her brother, she was expected to be more the mature one, the sensible one, while people made excuses like boys will be boys for her brother.

In any normal situation, she would have embodied a character many times bigger than herself, distracting Tommy from his anxiety, or distracting everyone else.

Since acting out a great storyteller circus ringmaster is what got them in trouble, she was uncharacteristically at a loss for what to do.

She'd seen her grandpa angry before—like the time she answered back after being told not to swing a broom around indoors. With reluctant hindsight, it was only once she knocked a picture off the wall and broke its glass that she admitted to herself this was perhaps a reasonable request.

Lyndsay had also seen Grandpa get angry at her dad countless times, usually when Dad told him not to climb ladders to clean leaves from his rain gutters. This made a certain sense to her; Grandpa didn't like being told what to do.

Both occasions were water droplets in a raging river compared to how angry Grandpa was now.

The children scurried out of the room, more mouse-like than pig, and silently agreed to play in the garden.

Lyndsay's face felt hot with embarrassment, shame, and guilt. The guilt surprised her, and inwardly she interrogated why she felt like that. For touching the belongings without asking? For getting anxious Tommy into trouble?

A quiet part of her knew it's because she touched the Storytelling Hat, and she felt terrible that Grandpa shouted at Tommy for it.

Lyndsay knew she wasn't supposed to touch the hat, it being so ancient and precious to her grandpa.

It wasn't like I'd break it, she sulked.

***

The sun felt surprisingly warm for December. Every morning when she'd woke up, Lyndsay had been eagerly checking out the window in case the world was covered with a fluffy blanket, but it was getting worrying close to Christmas so she'd had to settle for hard frosts.

On this one day, though, she was glad for the sun. If she'd been stuck inside following that telling off, she'd probably have started scratching the furniture or climbing the curtains.

Running her hand over the rough walls of Grandpa's old pebble-dashed house, by touch alone she noticed a stone was missing here or there, and sometimes one stone moved slightly. Lyndsay would then worry at the stone until it came loose in her hand.

Once she pried a stone from the wall, she immediately lost interest. Instead of being unique in a sea of fixed objects, it became a tiny, dirty bit of rock, and she'd dropped it on the ground. After several minutes of this, the tips of her fingers very slightly grazed from the rough walls, Lyndsay turned her attention to her big brother.

Tommy was hitting at the overgrown weeds with a stick with almost no effort to move or lift his arms. He was holding a thin dead branch that had fallen off one of the twisted, knobbly trees in Grandpa's garden. Finding a stick of her own, Lyndsay challenged Tommy to a swordfight.

With an impromptu '*En garde!*' she didn't need to explain to him they were pirates; her command enough to instantly immerse Tommy in her fantasy world.

As they fought—Lyndsay carefully trying only to hit Tommy's sword, never his hands—she explained she was a pirate queen and the fearsome Blackbeard wanted her treasure.

Tommy had heard of Blackbeard, obviously. But he was unsure girls could be pirates, let alone pirate queens.

Girls could be princesses, and princesses became queens, but he didn't see how or why queens would be pirates.

'You can't be both queen and a pirate!' he said at last.

'I'm not queen and a pirate, I'm the queen of the pirates!' Lyndsay shot back. 'I'm black-hearted Grace, the most feared pirate of all!'

'Girls can't be pirates!'

Lyndsay accidentally-on-purpose whacked Tommy's sword-fighting hand with her stick, making him yelp in pain.

'Sorry, missed. I am a girl, and I am a pirate, so that's that. I'm pirate queen black-hearted Grace, and I'm here for your pirate treasure!'

Occasionally, as they fought and shouted and laughed, Lyndsay would see Grandpa in the kitchen window. She didn't stop the game or turn to look, but she kept noticing him—and he couldn't be washing up every time.

Lyndsay did her best to show how much she didn't care by never acknowledging him.

Grandpa said get out of his sight, so we did, and it's not like we can play in the street or we'd be even more trouble.

She and Tommy had kept up their end of the bargain, so it was hardly her fault if Grandpa could see her through the window.

***

In the months that followed the awful day in the Christmas holidays, Lyndsay didn't know what to do with her hands or where to look when Grandpa wore the Storytelling Hat. Each time he put it on, she wondered if the Storytelling Hat might be angry and tell everyone stories about her.

If it is a magical hat, there's no telling what stories it knows about you, said a little voice inside Lyndsay's head who liked to stir trouble. *It might see everything, like Santa.*

And so, with the constant guilt of what the hat could tell her, and the memory of her grandpa's anger still so fresh, it was a complete surprise to Lyndsay when she was given the hat on her birthday. Little did she know, she wasn't the first choice to receive it.

Behind the scenes, Lyndsay's dad had been working on convincing his own dad to let the young girl have the Storytelling Hat for three years.

Grandpa resisted the suggestion at first, arguing that Lyndsay was flighty and wouldn't take care of it properly, that she didn't appreciate the importance of a good story, and even that girls don't wear top hats.

The truth was his feelings were hurt. Grandpa was tied to tradition—and tradition said the hat was to go to his oldest grandchild. That's why on his eleventh birthday, Grandpa presented the hat to Tommy—only for the boy to reject his gift.

Tommy had said he didn't want a dusty old hat. He didn't tell stories, and it was common knowledge that he didn't enjoy reading, not when he could watch YouTube or Netflix or play games.

Tommy's rejection was like a punch to the stomach for Grandpa. Receiving the hat more than 60 years before had been a great honour for him, and Tommy's rejection of the gift confirmed everything he thought was wrong with the modern world—and young people.

He was more than reluctant when his son suggested giving the hat to Lyndsay. The Storytelling Hat had never been given to a young girl, let alone a girl who wasn't even the oldest grandchild. But, eventually, his genuine affection for his granddaughter and an appreciation of her irregular imagination helped convince him, even if he briefly considered secretly giving her a duplicate hat.

***

Lyndsay's parents have two definite rules for the Storytelling Hat: she's never to take it out of the house, and she's always to put it back safely on top of her wardrobe when she finishes telling its stories.

The one and only exception is that Lyndsay can take the hat if they're visiting family—but only if they go by car. She still can't wear it if they go on a walk, or if she wants to play outside, and there is no way she's taking it on the Tube—that would be asking for all the wrong kinds of attention.

***

Lyndsay's own reputation as a master storyteller comes so quickly that it's easy to forget that the magical hat hasn't always belonged to her.

At first, aunts and uncles reluctantly agree to hear her stories—mistakenly thinking Lyndsay will lazily retell stories from her books or trot out tiresome tales of unicorns and fairies.

Instead, the hat helps expand the rough landscape of Lyndsay's imagination, and the stories the young girl tells almost the equal of her grandpa's. Though she might lack the variety of stories from her own life to share and some of the finer points of crafting narratives, she's never short of a dramatic plot.

Every evening, Lyndsay puts on her Storytelling Hat and tells a story for her family. A generous indulgence quickly becomes something her parents look forward to, and Lyndsay loves the spotlight more than ever.

Tommy, however, doesn't enjoy hearing his little sister's stories, nor does he enjoy enforced family time when he could be gaming. Most of all, the increased attention this gives Lyndsay feels about as welcome to him as a jagged toenail snagging on his socks.

Once, Lyndsay had looked up to Tommy, wanting to be part of whatever he was doing; now, she is more interested in books and stories.

Tommy is glad his sister doesn't repeat the ridiculous performance she adopted when they were so angrily shouted at by Grandpa but still hates everything about the hat.

***

Lyndsay loves the Storytelling Hat more than anyone expected. While her grandpa isn't himself without the Storytelling Hat, everyone was aware that he'd also noticeably lost the passion to tell its stories in recent years. And when Grandpa moves into sheltered housing, not long after Lyndsay's birthday, her parents are quietly glad the hat can't be lost.

The 11-year-old girl turns 12, and then 13, but her passion for telling stories doesn't diminish, and Lyndsay frequently has a precarious pile of books from the local library on her bedside table.

Although her storytelling matures as she better understands what good story telling involves—as opposed to writing—as far as anyone can tell, Lyndsay doesn't copy or take direct inspiration from the fictional worlds she spends so much time wandering through.

Animals are common in her stories, and her audiences are confident that an appearance of a dingo or a bear or a zebra will be significant—though it's impossible to predict how or where or when. The most common aspect of her stories is that they seem to have nothing in common with each other, and they all reflect a maturity beyond her years.

Sometimes, when her parents hear a story they later wonder aloud to each other how Lyndsay knows about the hussars of 18th Century Hungary.

Other times, someone openly questions if stories involving human sacrifice in Mesoamerican culture are perhaps a bit dark for a young girl, or how appropriate the themes are for visiting aunts enjoying the chocolate cake baked earlier in the day.

All of this makes her parents glad of their rule about not taking the hat to school.

Lost in her imagination, Lyndsay isn't the most popular child in school, or even her class, but she doesn't want to be like anyone else, girl or otherwise. And anyone who cares about her takes her as she is—because there's no other choice.

***

Lyndsay's stories bitterly remind Tommy of how he refused the hat.

Tommy doesn't believe in childish things like magic, and he certainly doesn't believe in magic hats. Magic is kids' stuff, a phrase he too-readily applies to almost anything he liked more than 6 months ago.

The hobbies he does have include leaving elaborately insulting comments on viral videos on YouTube, and whenever he hears the word *story* on TikTok. If he learns a film he enjoys is a book adaptation, Tommy immediately loses interest and will then say he hates it. The more anyone encourages him to read, the more reasons he has to hate books.

The rabbits in Tommy's stomach don't go away as he grows up, and he's no less prone to bouts of sickness putting him in bed for days, or even a week, but the teenager also develops a darkness, as if he feels like he's being denied something owed to him.

Though Tommy doesn't say it out loud, or specify what this mysterious thing is he's supposedly being denied, that doesn't douse the burning inferno of injustice that appears to burn inside him. This fire is easier to bear for him than feeling anxious.

Despite a general uncertainty about why he thinks his life is unfair, Tommy becomes a hostile neighbour to his sister. Once, it had felt like he'd adored the exuberant girl and that he'd wanted to be extroverted and imaginative like her; now he seemed almost ashamed of how he was in comparison.

Lyndsay used to include him in her wildly imaginative games, and most importantly she looked up to him as her older brother. That changed with her hat. *Not that I'd want to play make-believe games with a little girl anyway*.

Tommy wondered why Lyndsay wasn't like ordinary people who want to play real games, like *Call of Duty* or *Borderlands*. But he couldn't interest her in these games any more than she could engage him in the lives of kings and monsters and their destinies.

But most of all, Tommy resented Lyndsay because she stole his hat.

The hat was his first, and even if he didn't want it, in Tommy's world that didn't change that it was still rightfully his.

Lyndsay notices the changes in her older brother, though gradual. He more readily shouts and throws things at her now. But what Lyndsay doesn't notice is that Tommy resents her, specifically.

***

As well as telling stories, Lyndsay often immerses herself in writing fiction, though she only shares these stories online under elaborate pen names. These aren't Storytelling Hat stories. To her, the difference between the two is obvious, though she struggles to articulate it. Obviously, she makes up her own stories, while Storytelling Hat stories come from the hat.

For the tales she *writes*, she is simply a lightning rod—the stories already exist in the air around her, and she merely conducts them down onto the page.

But she doesn't write the Storytelling Hat stories—although that's not to say those stories are true, or that she thinks they're true. But the ways they come to her, and the way she tells them, feel different.

***

On the day of her grandpa's funeral, things start going very badly wrong.

The rule about not taking the Storytelling Hat out of the house still stands. No, attending a funeral is not the same as visiting family, she's told, even if the hat was once Grandpa's.

Funerals aren't the time for elaborate top hats, or for Lyndsay to tell stories. It's a day with more weighty concerns, and Lyndsay's parents compromise that Lyndsay can bring the hat out at home afterwards, since some family members are coming for the wake at their house.

There is an added condition that her stories have to be appropriate—*no stories about death*, and definitely *nothing about zombies*.

Lyndsay considers arguing this point—there was once a time that Grandpa would impishly have loved to tell a story about zombies to mourners after a funeral—but she thinks better of it.

Sitting in a cold, echoing church, Lyndsay knows not to question out loud why the funeral is there, even though Grandpa wasn't the churchgoing type.

It's the same church where Grandma is buried, and she supposes it makes a certain sense. She also chooses not to ask if it was what Grandpa wanted. Surely, the dead don't care one way or the other. Unless they're zombies, then they mostly care about moaning and eating brains.

Lyndsay's parents are appalled that they almost need to insist that Tommy comes to the funeral. Worse than a funeral for Tommy is the idea of people coming back to their house, and his parents expecting him to make small talk with relatives about school, what he wants to do for a living, and what he wants to study at university.

What they're interested in is as meaningless to him as what the pigeon outside his bedroom thinks about, or if it thinks at all.

Perhaps that's why he gets his idea for the Storytelling Hat.

***

As the adults prepare various items of food and an oversupply of drinks back at the house, the mood quickly becomes almost like a party.

People are telling funny stories about Grandpa, and they're even smiling and laughing at stories where Grandpa behaved shockingly badly.

Tommy's parents are too preoccupied to notice why their teenager isn't arguing about why he can't stay in his room.

***

Lyndsay knows to ask permission before bringing out the Storytelling Hat today, and sensibly recognises pushing her luck will land her in serious trouble.

She approaches her Mum, who is desperately trying to make sure everything is right, and Lyndsay recognises when she's trying to hold everything together—but amazingly she agrees straight away when Lyndsay asks if she can bring down the Storytelling Hat.

That distracted 'yes' is good enough for Lyndsay.

When she gets upstairs, the hat isn't in its dedicated spot on top of her wardrobe, and Lyndsay feels like she's inexplicably in a stranger's house.

The box is there, but it's empty. It doesn't make any sense.

Lyndsay tries to remember if she's taken it somewhere, or moved it and forgotten, but she'd know if she had. She runs back down to the kitchen.

'Mum, it's not there.'

Lyndsay's Mum is struggling with opening a bottle of wine. 'What isn't where? Look, help me a second. Hold this', Lyndsay's Mum hands the girl the bottle and a tea towel. How the tea towel is involved, Lyndsay is unclear.

'No, put that down, now give that back.' The wine bottle is taken away again. The kitchen feels much too hot.

'The Storytelling Hat, Mum. It's not there.'

'OK, well, maybe you can skip the stories for now.'

'But my hat!'

'Forget about the hat, love. I don't have time for this right now.'

Lyndsay wisely doesn't push the issue and quickly leaves the kitchen just as her Mum successfully pulls the cork from the bottle intact, like a rabbit from a hat.

Lyndsay knows if she doesn't leave now, her Mum will have her go around the wake asking everyone if they want anything.

After a few drinks, the same people always think they're comedians when they hear this question. *A million pounds*, they'll typically say—and Lyndsay isn't allowed to be sarcastic to relatives.

Tommy is lurking outside the kitchen. 'It's gone', he says.

'What do you mean? What are you talking about?' Lyndsay has a horrible feeling she does know what he's talking about.

'Your stupid hat. It went with Grandpa.'

'It did not. Don't lie. It was here yesterday.'

Lyndsay hasn't worn the hat since the weekend; it could have been missing for a couple of days, but she knows Tommy doesn't know that.

'It's a *magical* hat, and it *magically* went with him.' Tommy emphasises the word *magic* like he might say *fairies*.

'When they cremate Grandpa, the hat's toast.'

The question of what might happen to the hat after Grandpa died has already crossed Lyndsay's mind more than once at 3 am.

Lyndsay knows her Mum and Dad will be angry if she brings up the subject, like she only cares about the hat, but what if the stories stop? What if the hat disappears?

Deep down, Lyndsay feels like the Storytelling Hat knows she isn't its rightful owner. She knows now that Grandpa offered it to Tommy first—Tommy spitefully told her a few months ago—though she doesn't understand the significance of his refusal, or how it felt.

Lyndsay doesn't know if this means the hat still rightfully belongs to Grandpa.

The thought of Grandpa's cremation is too much, and Lyndsay starts to cry quietly. Tommy only smiles spitefully; Lyndsay is always so much sunshine.

Besides, he knows exactly where the hat is. After Lyndsay went to sleep, he crept into her room and took it. Now it's under his bed.

It's a month before anyone else sees the hat.

***

Tommy doesn't know what he plans to do with the hat, now that he has it. Maybe he'll throw it in the bin. Perhaps he'll keep it hidden under his bed. The important thing was taking it away and hurting his sister.

After the suggestion that Lyndsay has somehow lost it, taking it out of the house when she wasn't supposed to, her parents' explanation is Tommy must have moved it.

Denying it when they ask, he shouts at Lyndsay when she demands to know what he's done with it.

But even though Lyndsay looks like a kicked dog, keeping the hat hidden doesn't bring him the satisfaction he'd hoped.

***

One morning, Lyndsay notices a mysterious folded page of white paper, pushed under her bedroom door.

It isn't like her parents would communicate by note, and Tommy barely speaks to her, so why is he writing her notes, like he's still 12?

The note isn't a note at all but a ransom letter.

This is more creative than Lyndsay gives Tommy credit for. But any charitable thoughts quickly burn in a white-hot furnace.

WE HAVE YOUR HAT read the mismatched magazine letters.

Lyndsay supposes her brother has finally found a use for the magazines he collects, though her friend Suzie suggested he probably hides porn among the magazines because that's what her brother does.

Lyndsay chooses not to think about that and so deliberately never looks through the magazines. She isn't interested in supercars or men's fitness and definitely doesn't want to see any pictures of naked girls he's saved off the internet, printed and then hidden in there.

Lyndsay is almost relieved. Of course Tommy has the hat. Where else could it go? And if Tommy has the Storytelling Hat, then it's safe.

IF YOU WANT TO SEE IT AGAIN PUT £500 IN ENVELOPE IN TOP DRAWER SPARE ROOM. TELL NO ONE OR THE HAT DIES.

Tommy's an idiot, she thinks. For a start, he doesn't say when he wants the money, and he can't demand it without admitting the letter is from him. And he's greedy: if he asked for £100, she'd go along with it. She'd be mad, but it'd be worth it to get the Storytelling Hat back.

£500 is ridiculous. Nobody she knows could lend it to her; her parents certainly won't give it to her. At least, she decides, he also won't throw the hat away if he thinks he can get £500 out of her.

***

'You're a buffoon, Tom', Lyndsay tells her brother the next day, when their parents are out.

'And you're a little bitch,'

It's not the first or last time Lyndsay hears this insult, from Tommy or from anyone else, and she doesn't flinch. Last week, a boy in Tommy's year called her a frigid bitch because she didn't smile on command.

Tommy doesn't know what buffoon means, though he's pretty sure it sounds like a homophobic slur, and he knows he's not gay. Or maybe it's an animal? Like a buffalo, or a baboon. Maybe it's a mix of two animals? Could a buffalo have babies with a baboon?

Tommy resolves to search for answers later. But whatever a buffoon is, he knows it's not a compliment.

'I'm not giving you £500. You're an idiot if you think I am.'

'Who said anything about giving me your money?'

Lyndsay is unsure if her brother is really this dense. Does Tommy think she'll believe the Storytelling Hat is being ransomed by someone else? She can't tell if he's serious or not.

'So, you didn't send me a ransom demand for £500?'

'Nope.'

'You don't seem surprised. You didn't even ask what the note is for.'

'Because I don't care about your stupid hat.'

'Tom, I didn't say anything about the Storytelling Hat. You really are an imbecile. Give it back, or I'll tell Mum.'

'You think you're clever, don't you? You think big words make you smart but you're thick as shit. If you tell on me, I'll throw your stupid hat in the bin. Anyway, the hat's mine. Grandpa gave it to me first; it belongs to me.'

'That's not how anything works and you know it, Tommy. You've no right to take it and I want it back.'

Despite projecting the confidence of an emperor, Lyndsay isn't sure of herself. Maybe it is how things work? Or how it works with magical hats? But if she doesn't know, then Tommy doesn't either.

Standing in the doorway, she hesitates over what to do next. She can't search his room for the hat, and though she's tried looking over his shoulder, even Tommy isn't silly enough to leave it out in plain sight.

'If you're not giving me money, can you just get lost?'

'I thought you said you didn't send that note?'

'Your face makes me want to throw up. I never said I sent nothing. I said get lost if you aren't giving me money. You're the one who's talking shit about giving me 500 quid.'

'I AM NOT GIVING YOU ANY MONEY!' Lyndsay pictures herself as an ice queen of indifference, but he pushes her buttons.

Satisfied at her outburst, Tommy pushes his sister backwards out of the room and shuts the door in her face.

Neither of them have locks on their bedroom doors, but Lyndsay knows nothing good will happen if she barges back in.

'I AM NOT GIVING YOU ANY MONEY!' she screams at the door.

There's a thump as something hits the wall at head-height.

A short time later, her parents return home from whatever boring things they do, and Lyndsay hears them talking to Tommy in the kitchen. They're probably talking about his latest school report, or how much time he spends gaming with friends, but Lyndsay recognises an opportunity.

Interrupting the conversation in progress, Lyndsay asks her mum if she can borrow some money.

'Do you mean *have* some money? Or do you plan to give it back?'

Tommy's venomous glare would have worried a snake.

'I could wash the car?' Lyndsay suggests, knowing her parents hate it when she washes the car because of how she can't reach across the roof properly and gets so easily distracted.

'Is it for school? How much do you need?'

'About... £500?'

The look Lyndsay gets from her mum has her quickly backtracking, reassuring her Mum that she's just joking, that she only needs £50 for an English Lit conference.

Tommy is looking murderous, and Lyndsay reconsiders if this was a smart idea.

Usually, Lyndsay knows she can rely on her parents if she's in trouble, even if quarrels with her brother are kept between them, but she doesn't know what to do this time.

She's fairly sure Tommy wouldn't throw the hat away, especially if he's insisting it's his, but he's unpredictable and spiteful, and it all feels like too much of a risk.

Promising to get her Mum details of the trip, Lyndsay hastily retreats towards her bedroom—followed by Tommy.

On the landing at the top of the stairs, Tommy grabs his sister's arm.

'I know what you're trying to do, you little grass.'

Lyndsay thinks he looks like an ugly poisonous toad.

'Give me back what's mine, then.'

'It's mine now. Give me what I want and you can have it.'

'I don't have £100.'

Lyndsay is almost close to pleading. If Tommy wants to feel like a big man, she'll let him, just to get her hat back. Sometimes standing her ground only makes things worse.

'That's not my problem. I want it before Monday. And if you think you can tell Mum and Dad, I'm going to chop up the hat into little bits and then throw it in the bin.'

Tommy stalks out, and Lyndsay debates if she prefers it now he's stopped pretending he doesn't have her hat.

***

Before the weekend, Lyndsay gets another note under her door. Why Tommy is pretending again it's not him she doesn't try to fathom, but all the note says is: *IF YOU WANT HAT WE WANT MONEY.*

Lyndsay wonders if this is the most Tommy has ever written outside of school in his life, then remembers how once he used to write stories of his own, a long time ago. Long before arguments about hats.

One Christmas, the two of them wrote and performed a glove puppet play for their family. Tommy must have been about 7 at the time.

Even if Tommy is becoming a prolific writer of ransom notes, he's unlikely to go back to writing stories. But what if he does keep the Storytelling Hat for himself and his stories are better than hers?

After a couple of attempts at getting the hat to *do* something, Tommy loses interest in it completely. Whatever the story is with the stupid old thing, magic or not, he doesn't care.

Lyndsay obviously can't get the money and isn't going to try, so Tommy considers bargaining. He could make her do all his share of the housework for a year, or take whatever money she can beg, borrow or steal, but dismisses both for making him look weak.

He can't back down now. He needs to insist on the whole £500 or she'll never respect him, and she's disrespected him for too long.

On Sunday, Tommy invites Lyndsay to go look at a demolished house around the corner.

While he's not friendly, he's also not actively hostile, and Lyndsay supposes if she meets him halfway maybe they can pretend this didn't happen and he can give her back the Storytelling Hat without drama.

Sharing with their mum and dad where they're going and why, their parents are quietly grateful the pair seem to have got over whatever it is they are arguing about—and don't raise any objections or give any instructions, other than not to be too long, and not to go into the building site.

Lyndsay puts on a warm jacket. Tommy feels the need to act tough and is wearing shorts, so he doesn't bother with a jacket at all. Together they head out.

The Greenwich afternoon air has a bite, though Lyndsay is disappointed she can't see her breath and so can't joke about being a dragon. There's a lingering smell of smoke in the air, and a promise—or threat—of rain.

Tommy doesn't try to make conversation as they walk, answering monosyllabically to almost anything she asks.

'Have you run out of your magazines to cut out yet, Tom?' she asks.

'Shut up.'

Lyndsay thinks of a Venus fly trap and immediately regrets making any reference to the past week.

Reaching the demolished house, the two stand and look at the rubble silently. Lyndsay wonders what her brother is thinking and attempts conversation again.

'Hey, Tom, remember the time the dog that lived here got out? And when you caught it and took it back the owners didn't even know it had got out?'

Lyndsay remembers that day so well, how it had been only the two of them, like today. There'd been a storm and they wanted to look at what had changed. The dog must have got out when a fence blew down.

'Shut up.'

Lyndsay feels like Tommy is worse than usual.

Her brother picks up a piece of brick and throws it into the rubble, where a couple of weeks before there had been a house, with people moving between rooms, like it was some fixed point in time and space.

She wonders if Tommy aimed his throw at the rusty metal barrel, the only thing standing upright in the rubble. It looks like he isn't trying to hit anything, more like he only feels like throwing something.

Tommy turns suddenly to Lyndsay. 'Do you have my money?'

Lyndsay's heart drops to her shoes. He hasn't decided to move on at all; he only wanted to get her out of the house where their parents couldn't hear. 'I told you! I don't have it, I can't get it, and even if I did, or I could, I wouldn't give it to you.'

Tommy grunts, sounding like a stubborn ox, and looks away. Picking up another lump of brick, this time he throws it decisively at the barrel, and misses. 'Do you want to see your stupid hat?'

'What? Yes! Of course, I want it back! Are you going to give it back?'

'I'll show you your hat and what happens when you don't respect me.'

Lyndsay hates it when Tommy talks about 'respect'. Half the time he talks about how respect must be earned, that he gives respect to people only when they have done something worthy of it. The rest of the time he complains about not being respected, as if by virtue of being born a boy he deserves more respect.

Tommy walks towards the rusty barrel without speaking, and Lyndsay hesitates. It's unclear if she's meant to follow, or go home without him.

If she follows, will he take that as a sign that she's a meek lamb and he's a superior wolf? But if she goes home her parents will want to know why she's alone, and if Lyndsay admits she argued with Tommy, they'll ask her what it's about, if it's the same thing they've been arguing about for weeks.

Better to see what Tommy is doing and talk to him.

Standing by the barrel, Tommy is staring into it, as if fixated on his reflection in a pond. Lyndsay walks to his side and looks inside, but all she sees are old magazines.

She was worried for a moment, when Tommy asked about the hat, but there's only rubbish in the barrel. It's his stupid bike magazines, though she thinks she can see something glossy and porno-looking underneath.

Kicking over bricks and bits of wood, Tommy uncovers a box of matches. Lyndsay notices some cigarettes but says nothing. It's not worth aggravating him further.

Tommy tries to strike a match against the side of the box, but it snaps in two instead of lighting. With a noise like an unreliable car that won't start, he throws the broken match into the barrel, unlit. A second attempt, and the match very briefly flames before going out. He mumbles something without looking at his sister.

'What?'

'Are you deaf as well as stupid? I said, *have you got a lighter*?'

'No! Of course not. I don't smoke! Why would I have a lighter?'

Lyndsay suspects Tommy is saying something else under his breath when she hears what sounds like useless runt.

Her brother kicks around the bricks for a minute more, and Lyndsay wonders if he might be looking for a secret tunnel, before Tommy decides to go back to the matches.

The third match lights and burns strongly, slightly singeing Tommy's fingers before he throws it into the barrel. For a second, nothing happens and Lyndsay wonders if the match burnt out before it could light anything, or if the magazines are damp.

'Let's go home, Tom?'

At that moment, the magazines start to burn and it's the first time Lyndsay has seen her brother's smile in weeks.

'No, you'll want to watch this.'

There's a grim light in Tommy's eyes, like the owner of a cruel torture device.

Before Lyndsay wonders why watching burning magazines would interest an evolved human, she notices something. The magazines aren't stacked like she thought, they're leaning against something. *On top of something.*

Suddenly she's fighting the urge to be sick. She tries telling herself it's *not* the Storytelling Hat, but she can't look away. The feather burns and disintegrates and as the fabric chars the smell is like a mix of hot glue and burning sugar.

The acidic stenchl jolts something loose in Lyndsay, and as she turns and runs from the building site, she starts to sob.

Tommy doesn't try to stop her or say anything. He watches until the hat is unrecognisably burnt, then sits in the rubble, smoking a cigarette. He won't get £500 now, but this is pretty good. The hat is gone; now nobody can have it.

***

Lyndsay is crying uncontrollably when she gets home, and at first her parents think maybe something has happened to Tommy.

'No', she says. 'Tommy burnt it!'

Her parents exchange confused and concerned looks.

'What has Tommy burnt?' her mum asks. Trying to get sense out of Lyndsay is difficult.

Through her sobs she tries saying *you don't care*, but it makes things worse when her parents think they hear something involving the word *bear*.

Their relief to finally understand their inconsolable teenager only upsets her more. How can they be happy that Tommy burnt the Storytelling Hat! Her Storytelling Hat! *Grandpa's* Storytelling Hat!

***

Despite being relieved that Tommy isn't injured, his parents are sitting in a shared, furious silence in the living room when Tommy comes home an hour later.

By this time, Lyndsay has shut herself in her bedroom, further enraged that her parents were angrier about Tommy's smoking and them hanging about on a building site after he'd been specifically told to stay away.

Tommy admits he's been ignoring his parents' text messages—after all, only old people send SMS —and he acts like nothing they can do will bother him.

Until they change the WiFi password.

***

For Lyndsay, it isn't just about losing the Storytelling Hat because of the hat itself, but because it was the best gift she'd ever received, and because she knew what it meant to her grandpa. She didn't always like him; he could be as rude, unkind, and mean as an angry goose, but she also remembers how kind and loving he was, and how his stories were like gifts.

It felt like all of that had burnt with the hat. The hat was hundreds of years old! Passed down from grandparents since ... whenever top hats were invented, which Lyndsay is sure was a very long time ago. Possibly a thousand years.

Her parents still don't understand. To her, they're acting like Tommy burnt any old piece of her clothing, and Mum got mad when Lyndsay said she didn't want to go to school on Monday because she was too upset about the hat.

Tommy is more difficult to be around now that he can't get online, and he isn't about to go to the library to do it.

He is grounded, so he can't go to anyone else's house, and he has to come straight home from school, but he's unclear if he is grounded for burning a stupid hat, because he didn't come home for an hour and wouldn't reply to any stupid texts, or because stupid Lyndsay had grassed on him for smoking.

At least, he presumes she has, but all his parents ranting was a lot of words and he really doesn't care.

***

A week later, Lyndsay's Dad knocks on her bedroom door while she's reading a book called Imago. Lyndsay has been reading the trilogy that the novel concludes for weeks, and while he knows better than to interrupt her in the middle of a chapter he's also carrying a new top hat.

Lyndsay is speechless at first, and her dad mistakes it for gratitude. Moving to hug his daughter, she pulls away in disbelief.

The normally eloquent 13-year-old struggles to articulate her shock that he thinks this hat can simply replace the Storytelling Hat. But her dad has had time to think of a fitting analogy.

'Do you remember in *The Princess Bride*, the Dread Pirate Roberts?'

Of course she does, she says, it's one of her favourite *really old books*. Lyndsay's dad chooses to let that comment slide.

'OK, what does Westley say?'

'He says he inherited the ship from the Dread Pirate Roberts, who wasn't the real Dread Pirate Roberts either, and that the name just gets passed on.'

'That's like the hat. Yours was the real Storytelling Hat, but it inherited the name from the real hat before it. There was once a storytelling hat, an old top hat that belonged to my granddad, but that got half-eaten by moths and soiled by an unneutered tom cat, so it got thrown out and a new hat was made. And so, this is now the Storytelling Hat, just like Westley is the real Dread Pirate Roberts.'

'Someone at school said there is a real-life Dread Pirate Roberts, called Rob or something?'

'That's not something we need to talk about. Let's think about making your hat instead. What do you think we should put on it?'

The two spend the next hour searching online for craft supplies and inspiration for making the Storytelling Hat.

***

One month on, and Tommy is free from being grounded. It's typical his parents release him on the weekend of his dad's 50th birthday when the extended family are visiting.

The usual various aunts and uncles arrive, and while it makes a change from only seeing them for weddings and funerals (although he finds christenings and baptisms most boring of all) Tommy resents having to stay home and make the same old conversation he always must; that hasn't changed since the last time he saw them all.

While he might not be grounded any more, Tommy also isn't yet entirely forgiven by his parents for his smoking—or for destroying Lyndsay's hat—so they watch him carefully and have him constantly checking all their guests have what they need.

As a contrast, Lyndsay is starting to feel herself again and knows that this family gathering will, at least, be very different from the dismal day of Grandpa's funeral.

While she and her Dad made the new Storytelling Hat together, she's wisely kept its existence a secret from her brother and nobody plans to tell Tommy the truth about the original.

A dozen possible different story ideas swirl about in Lyndsay's head as she approaches some of the extended family she likes the most. Of all her aunts and uncles and cousins, these most appreciate her unique imagination.

Lyndsay feels a narrative starting to coalesce. It's the story of a pirate queen who also happens to be a bear—people are more surprised that she's a woman than that she's a bear—and Lyndsay thinks this will be one of her best stories.

When Tommy sees Lyndsay come downstairs, wearing the Storytelling Hat, the rabbits in his stomach start doing backflips.

Retreating to the relative safety of the garden and other people, Tommy decides that if a hat somehow recovers from being burnt maybe it is magical after all—and he doesn't touch it again.

Ursa Major; or *an incomplete record of Earth's vulnerable bear species*

The Oorun invaders were sure they had it right. They wouldn't be embarrassed like some unprepared intergalactic nobodies.

They knew better than underestimating even their weakest enemies, but the token resistance the Oorun received gave humans approximately 90 minutes longer than they might have otherwise known.

Oorun intelligence was so beyond humans that Earth's nations didn't stop arguing long enough to unite against the threat.

Humanity was dissolved, disintegrated, dissected, desiccated and decimated.

Unliked other invasions, whose missions were once thwarted by microscopic life, the Oorun were prepared.

No viruses or microbes on Earth troubled them; no ubiquitous but deadly liquid, gas or solid substance concerned them.

It wasn't as if the Oorun were unprepared for other life on Earth, and their best minds were mostly correct.

One report suggested that its vast, global colonies of ants might, over time, be a concern—but they weren't an immediate worry. The Oorun had more in common with ants than with apes.

***

Reports of the Oorun's disastrous downfall correctly identify that Human Beings were wiped from the Earth quickly.

However, you may be familiar with the insistence from some corners of the cosmos that it was a coordinated effort by the planet's other species that was the invaders' undoing.

With magnificently misguided confidence, others assert that Earth's plant life unexpectedly and collectively fought back. Both are comically incorrect.

It's typical of beings like the Oorun to presume any encountered resistance is organised. The shame and surprise of their inglorious defeat has distorted the truth.

The Oorun travelled light years in ways that defy comprehension, and other pangalactic pilgrims struggle with how physics bends to the Oorun's will.

They knew what roamed Earth's surface and swam in its oceans. The Oorun's detailed taxonomy was beyond anything Earthlings could accomplish given a hundred thousand years.

In common with other failed interstellar invasions and aggressive manoeuvres, they over-emphasised organised resistance and technical advances—when they should have looked at the battles humanity was fighting with their own planet.

What doomed the Oorun was Earth's bears.

***

The Oorun spent a great effort securing and stabilising the planet.

In about one of Earth's days, the Oorun's conquered world was made safe in various ways. They established a stable climate, restored polar ice caps, replenished rainforests and rebalanced carefully Earth's fauna and flora populations, helping non-human forms of life to thrive.

They didn't expect what came next.

The Oorun released zoo animals with an abundance of caution—a creature kept in unnatural captivity, they reasoned, might behave unexpectedly. Encountering bears in the wild was entirely different.

The first bear they met was the giant panda. With the panda's flat face, large eyes and round, cuddly appearance, the Oorun were unprepared for the soft-looking bear's unbreakable grip. Many Oorun were savaged beyond all recognition. They then left the pandas in peace.

If their research had extended as far as the wild panda's mating habits, the Oorun might have chosen not to get close enough to experience its almost unrivalled crushing bite force.

***

The Arctic Tundra is as different from the temperate mountains of China as imaginable, but wide-scale Oorun losses to polar bears came from a simple misunderstanding.

They were unconcerned with fluffy white polar bears because of a galactic lost-in-translation moment with the word *vulnerable*.

Following habitat loss from climate change, the polar bear was classified as a vulnerable species. Instead of *at risk of extinction*, they were misunderstood as *weak and sensitive*.

After all, surely humans couldn't survive in Arctic environments with anything *threatening*.

***

Encountering polar bears (restored to population numbers unseen for centuries), the Oorun quickly discovered the bears were less vulnerable than the word suggested.

Technologically advanced enough to travel across—and possibly outside—the universe, the Oorun didn't have the opportunity for feasts in the bear's honour, as might have happened in earlier times on Earth. Instead, their explorers were a light snack for the enormous, hyper-carnivorous beasts.

Contemporary polar bear opinions on this aren't recorded, but subsequent researchers capable of communicating with Earth's wildlife have established polar bears considered the Oorun as less nourishing than seals, if easier to catch.

After cautiously surrendering the whole of China to its pandas, the Arctic was declared off-limits, too.

***

Shaken by now-global reports of bear fatalities, other groups of Oorun met koalas in Australia.

It was noted that while koalas were bad-tempered, they weren't a concern, and Australia was gloriously declared free from dangerous bears. Their research didn't extend to establishing that koalas aren't bears, and if the Oorun had left any humans alive, they might have heard of creatures known as *drop bears*.

Oorun scientists reassured everyone that no large predators lived on the island, oblivious to the hefty creatures living in the densely forested Great Dividing Range. The drop bear's nickname *death from above* didn't appear in their research, and the misleadingly named 'koala bears' left the Oorun themselves endangered.

The Oorun were massacred when the interstellar travellers foolishly ventured near something more dangerous than a black hole: Australia's closed-canopy forests and woodlands.

Oorun scouts investigating the forests and woods thought them a good place to set up a semi-permanent camp, until they fatally ignored movement in the canopy above them. In a blur of mottled orange fur, powerfully built animals, each nearly the size of leopards, ambushed their unsuspecting prey.

Immediately stunned by the impact of the falling drop bears, Oorun heads, for want of a better description, were bitten clean off by the large, predatory marsupials.

The remaining Oorun abandoned the entire continent.

***

Despite losing large parts of their new planet, the Oorun boldly tried establishing themselves throughout North America, South America, Asia, Africa and Europe.

Imagine if North America's brown bears had been more awake when the Oorun swiftly killed all humans. In another universe, the invaders might have used their reality-warping technology to leave before they arrived. As it was, when the northern half of the Earth started tilting towards Earth's Sun, the bears were waking up from hibernation and were groggy and hungry.

The Oorun took precautions in wooded areas, should drop bears be endemic across the planet, and remained sceptical of anything described as vulnerable. But their initial observations of brown and black bears were disastrously incomplete.

Gambolling cubs climbed trees while watched by their mothers, and solitary males intimidated other bears from fishing spots. These all seemed manageable, and even the Oorun had an aesthetic appreciation for how cute bears seemed.

The invaders began to drop to numbers that could be described as at risk.

As polar bears considered their visitors less nourishing than seals, their Kodiak cousins ranked them inferior to wild salmon—but an easy meal is rarely refused.

The losses suffered from both polar and drop bears, panda and grizzly bears, black and Kodiak bears, and even sloth bears (the latter another horrible mistake) risked the Oorun population's stability.

Concerns around what other bears might exist combined with many Oorun suffering violent encounters with domestic house cats and the whole invasion was scrapped.

A suggestion of relocating to Earth's Moon was dismissed when they discovered a secret Moonbase of intelligent armed bears. These bears, at least, were left in peace.

Douglas Adams, one of Earth's greatest philosophers, once referred to its location as '*the uncharted backwaters of the unfashionable end of the western spiral arm of the Milky Way.*'

Fashionable or not, the Oorun never returned.

The Last Storm

'Rain is holy water', she'd say. 'That's why it burns.'

When I asked, 'Why would holy water burn?' Mother changed the subject.

***

Right now, it feels like this storm of the century will last forever. Our power went out an hour ago, mobile networks 30 minutes later.

We're sheltering in the basement, listening to the rain. Down here, wedged next to the tumble drier, it smells like a mix of old fabric softener and WD-40.

You're curled up warm beside me, drifting between sleep and waking. You know you're safe, Starbuck.

I was keeping the emergency radio for ... emergencies. Don't waste the battery, I thought. But now I don't know if we'll survive tonight, and this oldies radio station is making me nostalgic.

There's no DJ on this station. A producer programmed its computer in advance, fleeing town yesterday before the roads clogged worse than our shower drain.

Smashing Pumpkins. L7. Hole. Screaming Trees. As they play, I write each band and track in this notebook, like lines from a spell.

This music will feel like ancient history to you when you're old enough to appreciate music. If we make it.

I haven't written down spells since you were born, Starbuck. I haven't looked in my mother's books. But I haven't burnt them, either. I haven't changed as much as I'd like to believe.

You're stirring in your sleep right now and I'm stroking your soft hair.

'It's OK, I have you', I whisper as the wind howls outside.

I don't say everything will be alright. I won't lie. And if we make it through this, I'll never lie to you again.

***

My mother was like you. The superstitious type.

She'd turn away if she saw a line of crows sitting on the fence. A black block of murder.

'He's watching', she'd mutter.

When I was your age, my grandmother—your great-grandmother Ursula—told me fantastic stories she'd heard from her grandmother. Stories about *Veles*, god of the forest. He could transform into any form but always appeared as a bear.

Granny Ursula swore she met Veles once, in bear form. I often wondered how she knew it was him.

She told the story in many forms, and rarely was it the same twice, but the key details never changed much. Granny Ursula was caught in a forest in a storm when she met an enormous bear.

Depending on when she told the story, sometimes the bear spoke to her and sometimes she just understood him. Either way, she knew it was Veles—and Veles led her safely to a cave where she sheltered until the storm passed.

Granny Ursula would offer wine to Veles, pouring a little out on the roots of a nearby Willow tree. I don't know when we stopped.

***

I don't know if you'll read this, Starbuck. I don't know if this once-in-a-lifetime storm will end our lifetime tonight. It feels like it has changed into something else.

I'm struggling to keep it together for you. If you knew how scared I feel, you'd be scared, too.

Outside the storm is worsening. I can hear roofs ripping off, trees snapping, uprooting and crashing. I don't know if the breaking glass just now was our windows or someone else's.

To stay calm, I'm repeating the brands from radio ads like a litany of saints: *Google. Apple. Tesla.*

Don't judge me, but I offered a quiet prayer to Veles. Any port in a storm, people say, Starbuck. Maybe he'll remember us?

It feels like everyone else has forgotten.

***

I don't know how long it's been. The batteries in the radio are dead and it's dark outside. A noise upstairs woke me, but you've barely stirred.

Someone is in the house. Maybe they broke in, looking for a port in a storm.

I can hear roaring; Starbuck, I am not making this up. It isn't human.

I've poured a little wine, like holy water, inside the basement door. I don't know if I meant it as offering or protection.

I don't know if the door will hold and I'm now writing this for anyone who might find it.

Would I know Veles if I met him?

Acknowledgments

Thank you to Amberley Laverick for the *Pen & Cake* writing group, where the bears first arrived. Thanks for the inspiration and encouragement and the opportunity to write just for the sheer joy of writing.

Thank you to Kirsten Thomson and Ellie Greenham and all the other writers of *Pen & Cake* who listened to my stories and gave me feedback and advice.

Thank you to Elaine Hanlon and Samantha Gibson-Mayne for welcoming me into your *Literarily Speaking* group; thank you for the encouragement and enthusiasm and kindness and always being willing to read a story on a deadline. Thank you for believing in me even when I didn't.

Thank you, also, to all the various members of *Literarily Speaking* for putting up with my stories about bears every time.

Thank you to Laura Keenan and Linda Martin of Night Parrot Press for the flash fiction workshops where ideas of stories about bears have often emerged, and for your own enthusiasm and encouragement

Thank you to the poets Leonard James and Ben Riddle for being great writers, good friends, and loyal, regular performers at *Words Wide Night*.

Thank you to Liz Tan for your regular correspondence, and for reading various story drafts. You're one of the most talented writers I know, as well as one of the most patient people and one of my kindest friends.

Thank you to Miriam Sullivan for reading my stories, and giving your most honest feedback, especially if that feedback is that something doesn't work for you.

Thank you to Rylee Jensen of Katmai National Park, Patricia Alessi, and David Gallagher for talking to me about your own real-life experiences with bears.

Endless thanks to all the editors who have published versions of stories from this book—and stories not in this book. Thanks for the platform, for your feedback, and for your encouragement and suggestions.

Thank you to S.E. Harsha for publishing a quirky story called *The Ring Bearer*, showing me that people could and would like my stories. Thank you also to Ellyn Parry for publishing my story *The Unbearable Wonder of Being Yourself* (that would become *The Moon Bear*), and thank you to Gregory Rowbotham for featuring the story *Ursa Major* on your podcast and being so willing to read and offer feedback on my stories.

Thank you to my various friends around the world, too many to list individually, who've listened to me talking about *Year of the Bear* for far too long. Special thanks to Amanda, Ceri, Caila, Calvin, Kath and Rachelle for always sending me random bear content.

Thank you to Sasha, for reading 'The Right to Arm Bears' and helping me with naming conventions to help me avoid looking like an idiot.

Thank you to Stuart M Buck of *Bear Creek Gazette* for being so generous with your time, advice, and feedback and expecting nothing in return.

Thank you to the various unknown editors of the various NYC Midnight competitions. You may never hear of this book but thank you all the same. Your honest feedback and things to improve have always buoyed me.

Thank you to Bob Goldsmith and Jacquelin Cangaro for your kind words and praise on the sample you saw for *Year of the Bear*—you helped me believe that maybe there was something to this.

Thank you to Samuel Field for turning this book into a reality. Without your belief in the bears, this book wouldn't exist. Thank you for the encouragement and advice and resources and conversations and endless patience, and for all the beers.

Thank you to Victoria Heath-Smith of Myriad Editions. Your help and hard work and enthusiasm and unrivalled skills turned this from being the scrappy, inconsistent and largely nonsensical ramblings of a bear-obsessed weirdo into a proper book (by a bear-obsessed weirdo.) Similarly, thank you to Shelby Newsom for your polishing and shining copy edits.

Thank you to Rabble Books for your excitement and support for this book.

Thank you to my family for your enthusiasm and excitement about this book, and encouraging a love of stories in me from an early age. It's safe to say if you hadn't instilled this love of stories, I wouldn't be writing my own today.

Above all, thank you Cass for reading all my stories and patiently listening to me talk about robot bears and were-bears and bears in space.

Thank you for discussing with me the ideas and jokes that would go on to become some of these stories.

Thank you for loving me and supporting me through the endless months of writing and revisions and editing, and for consoling me when everything feels dark.

This book is for you; though you'd probably rather I'd got a job instead.

***

Year of the Bear was written on the stolen lands of the Whadjuk people of the Noongar nation, and I pay my respects to Aboriginal elders, past and present.

I am a guest on this land and I acknowledge the continuing culture and the contribution that the Whadjuk people make to the life of this region, recognising that sovereignty was never ceded.

About the Author

Jay is an award winning author of contemporary fiction, folklore and science fiction with fantasy and social commentary to entertain, challenge, and sometimes frighten readers.

His fiction has unifying themes around culture and identity and has earned praise and recognition from many websites and organisations, including NYC Midnight, the Creatives Journal, WriteNow literary journal, Neuro Logical literary magazine, Press Pause, Love to Read Local, and Bear Creek Gazette.

The bears set up camp in Jay's imagination in 2019, and he hoped they'd leave him alone if he wrote stories about them. The bears then demanded a whole book, and Jay wisely agreed to let them have what they wanted and called it Year of the Bear.

Born and raised in England's homogeneous home counties, which have a surprising non-zero number of bear sightings, Jay studied at universities in Derby (UK) and Utah (USA). Jay then convinced Leicester's De Montfort University (and possibly himself) that he wasn't a frustrated novelist. They let him complete a post-grad in journalism. His journalism has been published on subjects as far-ranging as local news, exorcisms, music, astronomy, haunted houses, and street roller hockey.

When he's not working, Jay is usually found in the wild in Perth bookshops, or in various cafés and coffee shops, writing and making them look untidy. When he's not writing, Jay is generally fretting about how he really should be writing. His ADHD brain is filled with half-remembered lyrics from songs, lines from poems, quotes from films, and facts about bears, leaving no room to remember that thing he was meant to do today.

Jay's next book, Tales from Beyond the Bear-Proof Fence, is currently a work-in-progress. He hopes the bears will be satisfied after that and leave him alone.

After living in seven cities across three continents in the last 20 years, Jay now lives in Perth, Western Australia, with his fiancée and two boisterous cats. Jay still misses his family in the UK.

Publication Details

March of the Bears and The Ring Bearer were first published together as the story The Ring Bearer on Press Pause (2021)

The Moon Bear was first published as The Unbearable Wonder of Being Yourself on The Creatives Journal (2021)

Scared of Your Own Shadow was first published as Shadow of the Bear on Love to Read Local (2021)

A Summer's Tale was first published on PNH e-zine (2021)

Ursa Major was first broadcast on Wah Wonders Why (2021)

www.ingramcontent.com/pod-product-compliance
Lightning Source LLC
Chambersburg PA
CBHW071927130726
47909CB00014B/2600